YORK NOTES

AQA POETRY ANTHOLOGY: CHARACTER AND VOICE

NOTES BY GEOFF BROOKES

Longman
is an imprint of

PEARSON

York Press

YORK PRESS
322 Old Brompton Road, London SW5 9JH

PEARSON EDUCATION LIMITED
Edinburgh Gate, Harlow,
Essex CM20 2JE, United Kingdom
Associated companies, branches and representatives throughout the world

First published 2010

10 9 8 7 6 5 4 3 2 1

ISBN 978–1–4082–4874–4

Illustrations by John Dillow

Phototypeset by Border Consultants, Dorset

Printed in the UK

Quotations from: 'Checking Out Me History' copyright © 1996 by John Agard, reproduced by kind permission of John Agard c/o Caroline Sheldon Literary Agency Limited; 'The Clown Punk' by Simon Armitage, reproduced by permission of Faber & Faber, Ltd and David Godwin Associates; 'Give' from *The Dead Sea Poems* (Faber, 1995), copyright © Simon Armitage, 1995, reproduced by permission of David Godwin Associates; 'On a Portrait of a Deaf Man' from *Collected Poems*, by John Betjeman © 1955, 1958, 1962, 1964, 1968, 1970, 1979, 1981, 1982, 2001. Reproduced by permission of John Murray (Publishers). Excerpts from "Medusa" from THE WORLD'S WIFE (Picador, 1999) by Carol Ann Duffy. Copyright © 1999 by Carol Ann Duffy. Reprinted by permission of Faber and Faber, Inc., an affiliate of Farrar, Straus and Giroux, LLC., and Picador, an imprint of Pan Macmillan, London; 'Casehistory: Alison (head injury)' by U. A. Fanthorpe from *Collected Poems 1978–2003* (Peterloo Poets, 2005), reproduced by permission of R. V. Bailey; 'The Horse Whisperer' by Andrew Forster from *Fear of Thunder* reproduced by permission of Flambard Press; 'Brendon Gallacher' by Jackie Kay from *Darling: New & Selected Poems* (Bloodaxe Books, 2007) reproduced by permission of Bloodaxe Books; 'Les Grands Seigneurs' by Dorothy Molloy by permission of Faber & Faber, Ltd; 'Singh Song!' by Daljit Nagra reproduced by permission of Faber & Faber, Ltd; 'The River God' by Stevie Smith, from COLLECTED POEMS OF STEVIE SMITH, copyright © 1972 by Stevie Smith. Reprinted by permission of New Directions Publishing Corp. and the Estate of James MacGibbon; 'The Hunchback in the Park' by Dylan Thomas, from THE POEMS OF DYLAN THOMAS, copyright © 1943 by New Directions Publishing Corp. Reprinted by permission of New Directions Publishing Corp. and David Higham Associates.

CONTENTS

PART THREE
KEY CONTEXTS AND THEMES

PART FOUR
LANGUAGE AND STRUCTURE

PART FIVE
GRADE BOOSTER

PART ONE: INTRODUCTION

Study and revision advice

There are two main stages to your reading and work on *Character and Voice*. First, the study of the poems as you read them. Second, your preparation or revision for exam or controlled assessment. These top tips will help you with both.

 ### READING AND STUDYING THE CLUSTER – DEVELOP INDEPENDENCE!

- Try to engage and respond **personally** to the ideas and stories – not just for your enjoyment, but also because it helps you develop your own **independent ideas** and **thoughts** about the poems. This is something that examiners are very keen to see.

- **Talk** about the poems with friends and family; ask questions in class; put forward your own viewpoint – and, if time, **read around** the poems to find out about character and voice.

- Take time to **consider** and **reflect** on the **key elements** of the cluster; keep your own notes, mind-maps, diagrams, scribbled jottings about the poems and how you respond to them; follow the story of each poem as it progresses (what do you think might happen?); discuss the main themes and ideas that interested the poet (what do *you* think it is about? Change? Love? The past?); pick out language that impresses you or makes an **impact**, and so on.

- Treat your studying **creatively**. When you write essays or give talks about the cluster make your responses creative. Think about using really clear ways of explaining yourself, use unusual but apt **quotations**, well-chosen **vocabulary**, and powerful, persuasive ways of beginning or ending what you say or write.

 ### REVISION – DEVELOP ROUTINES AND PLANS!

- **Good revision** comes from good **planning**. Find out when your exam or controlled assessment is and then plan to look at key aspects of the cluster on different days or times during your revision period. You could use these Notes – see **How can these Notes help me?** – and add dates or times when you are going to cover a particular topic.

- Use **different ways** of **revising**. Sometimes talking about the poems and what you know/don't know with a friend or member of the family can help; other times, filling a sheet of A4 with all your ideas in different colour pens about a particular poem, for example 'Brendon Gallacher', can make ideas come alive; other times, making short lists of quotations to learn, or numbering events in the poem can assist you.

- **Practise plans** and **essays**. As you get nearer the 'day', start by looking at essay **questions** and writing short bulleted plans. Do several plans (you don't have to write the whole essay); then take those plans and add details to them (quotations, linked ideas). Finally, using the advice in **Part Five: Grade Booster**, write some practice essays and then check them out against the advice we have provided.

> **EXAMINER'S TIP**
>
> Prepare for the exam or controlled assessment! Whatever you need to bring, make sure you have it with you – books, if you're allowed, pens, pencils – and that you turn up on time!

Introducing *Character and Voice*

This cluster of poems deals with people and the things they say and do. What could be more interesting than that? We read poetry to find out what a poet has to say, to find out what made them express their thoughts in this form. However, sometimes poets do not speak as themselves. They adopt a different **persona** or **character** who then speaks in a voice different from their own.

This can give the poet great freedom. They can tell a story from the point of view of a character and then comment upon it themselves. They can explore feelings and emotions, they can reflect on experiences. They can give words to characters that they do not agree with, in order to enhance their creation. The poet might want us to draw conclusions about the difference between what they say and what they actually mean.

You get an immediate and deep insight into others by listening to the voices that are created in these poems. And we must never take these characters at face value. The poet never expected you to do that.

That is why these poems are so fascinating. The characters and their voices set up echoes in our minds and inspire responses that deepen our understanding of the poets' artistry and their intention. The poems repay close and careful study and provide fascinating insights. Read them and enjoy them!

Andrew Forster: 'The Horse Whisperer'

Still I miss them. Shire,
    Clydesdale, Suffolk.
The searing breath,
    glistening veins,
steady tread and the pride,
most of all the pride.

The horse whisperer was once a vital part of his community. He had a magical power over horses that led his community to respect and fear him in equal measure. We hear his voice in Andrew Forster's poem and we hear his pain at their rejection of him more acutely because *the horse whisperer speaks to us directly.*

John Betjeman: 'On a Portrait
of a Deaf Man'

And when he could not hear
me speak
He smiled and looked so wise
That now I do not like to think
Of maggots in his eyes.

Look at the way Betjeman describes his father in the poem. We can see that deafness was a key element of his character. That comes through clearly in the title of the poem. Even though he couldn't hear what Betjeman was saying, he seemed to have a wise understanding. He was deaf when he was alive and he remains so now that he is dead. It is the only part of him that is constant. Everything else about him has decayed. The poet's feelings are made clear both in the structure of the poem and in the words he uses.

Dylan Thomas: 'The Hunchback
in the Park'

That she might stand in the night
After the locks and chains

All night in the unmade park

The hunchback can't take his fantasy creation with him in the evening. The park is chained and locked, just like his dreams. It is a fantasy world that joins the hunchback and the boys, a place where you can escape from yourself for a short time. He has to leave the dream behind but it draws him back every day, in spite of the boys. The poet gives us insight by making us aware of the loneliness and isolation at the heart of the hunchback's life.

Introducing the poets

John Agard (b. 1949): 'Checking Out Me History'

Agard is a poet, short story and children's writer who was born in Guyana. He worked as a journalist before moving to England in 1977. He has toured schools promoting an understanding of Caribbean culture and became poet in residence at the BBC in London. He travels extensively performing his poetry.

Simon Armitage (b. 1963): 'Give' and 'The Clown Punk'

He was born in Huddersfield and worked as a probation officer and a supermarket assistant before he achieved success as a writer. He has won awards for his poetry and his song lyrics. During 2000 he was poet in residence at the Millennium Dome. He is lead vocalist with his band The Scaremongers.

John Betjeman (1906–84): 'On a Portrait of a Deaf Man'

He was born in Highgate in North London. He was a poet, a writer of guidebooks to English counties and a popular broadcaster on radio and television. He believed that English heritage should be preserved. He was knighted in 1969 and was made Poet Laureate in 1972.

Robert Browning (1812–89): 'My Last Duchess'

Browning was one of the leading Victorian poets. He was born in London and educated at home. He learnt many languages and was fascinated by Italy. He was also a talented musician. His courtship of and marriage to the poet Elizabeth Barrett is a particularly famous love story.

Carol Ann Duffy (b. 1955): 'Medusa'

She was born in Glasgow and brought up in Stafford. She was encouraged to write by her English teachers at school. She has received many awards for her work, which includes drama and work for children, as well as poetry. She has been awarded the OBE and the CBE. In 2009 she became Poet Laureate.

U. A. Fanthorpe (1929–2009): 'Casehistory: Alison (head injury)'

Ursula Fanthorpe was born in Kent. She was a successful English teacher but gave up that career to concentrate on her writing. She studied for a diploma in school counselling and later worked as a hospital clerk in Bristol. In 2001 she was made CBE for her services to poetry.

Andrew Forster (b. 1964): 'The Horse Whisperer'

Andrew Forster grew up in South Yorkshire. His poems and reviews appear in magazines and anthologies. His first collection of poems, *Fear of Thunder* (including 'The Horse Whisperer') was praised by critics. He works as a writer and facilitator.

Thomas Hardy (1840–1928): 'The Ruined Maid'

Hardy is remembered for his famous and popular novels, although he regarded himself as a poet. He was born near Dorchester and trained as an architect in London but returned home to write. He was always interested in social issues and had great sympathy for the lives of ordinary people.

Jackie Kay (b. 1961): 'Brendon Gallacher'

She was born in Edinburgh. Her mother was Scottish and her father Nigerian. She was brought up by adoptive parents. She worked in London as a cleaner and as a hospital porter. She is not only a poet but has also has been involved as a writer with theatre groups and has written for television.

Dorothy Molloy (1942–2004): 'Les Grands Seigneurs'

She was born in County Mayo in Ireland. She worked in Barcelona as a historical researcher and as a painter. She returned to live in Dublin but never saw a copy of her books. Her first volume of poetry appeared in 2004 a few months after her death. Two other volumes were published later.

Daljit Nagra (b. 1966): 'Singh Song!'

Daljit Nagra is a British poet who was born and brought up in West London and Sheffield. He was encouraged to write at university and has received the support of many established poets. He lives in London, and works as an English teacher.

Percy Bysshe Shelley (1792–1822): 'Ozymandias'

Shelley is now regarded as a major English poet though his work was not widely circulated in his lifetime. He was bullied at school and later expelled from university. He lived for a while on the continent and died when his boat sank in a sudden storm at sea off the coast of Italy. He is buried in Rome.

Stevie Smith (1902–71): 'The River God'

Florence Smith was born in Hull and was given the nickname 'Stevie' by a friend. She was very ill as a child, which prompted her fascination with death. She worked as a private secretary in a publishing company for thirty years. Her broadcasts for the BBC brought her popularity with other writers in her lifetime.

Dylan Thomas (1914–53): 'The Hunchback in the Park'

He was born in Swansea and worked for a while as a journalist for the local paper. Much of his writing reflects on his childhood experiences in Wales. He wrote stories and plays and became a script writer for public information films in the Second World War. His broadcasts and performances of his works were extremely popular.

Jackie Kay: 'Brendon Gallacher'

SUMMARY

❶ The speaker talks about her friend from childhood, Brendon Gallacher.

❷ She invented a complete biography for him with precise details.

❸ She convinces her mother of his reality.

❹ The speaker's mother questions her about his address.

❺ The fantasy of an imaginary friend is shattered and the illusion dies.

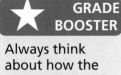

GRADE BOOSTER

Always think about how the poems deal with similar ideas. Look for connections between them.

WHAT IS SPECIAL ABOUT THIS POEM?

A It is a very successful **impression** of a **child's fantasy creation** reflected in her own words.

B The poem is very carefully **structured**.

C It gives us a convincing **picture** of Brendon Gallacher as a **real person**.

D A simple question **destroys** the fantasy creation.

E The poem's **themes** shows the death of **innocence** and the **fragility** of our dreams.

KEY QUOTE

'… his spiky hair, his impish grin, his funny, flapping ear.'

STRUCTURE AND VOICE

The poem is a fine example of how repetition can hold a poem together. Notice the repeated use of 'he' and 'his'. This puts Brendon Gallacher at the centre of the poem, especially after their use to start six of the first eight lines.

The poem doesn't use a conventional **rhyme** but every line ends in virtually the same sound, with the use of the letter 'r'. This gives it a sense of unity. The full name 'Brendon Gallacher' always appears at the end of a line. It gives the name a prominence and suggests the insistent repetition of a child. It also indicates that the image of Brendon Gallacher is constantly in the speaker's mind as she keeps the illusion alive.

The whole poem uses the **rhythms** of ordinary speech, which means that the voice of the poet is heard very clearly. At times it sounds like a child talking. For example the speaker always refers to him by using his full name as a child might. The length of the sentences is varied throughout. The repetition of the address '24 Novar', first as a question and then as a statement, is exactly what happens in everyday conversation. Jackie Kay's Scottish heritage is reflected in the details of the poem ('Glasgow' and 'burn' for example) and the accent used in the second verse. The word 'my' is used nine times, which shows that Brendon Gallacher doesn't belong to anyone else. The toy he is based upon is hers and so therefore is her fantasy. In fact her mother refers to him as 'your Brendon Gallacher'.

Brendon Gallacher

The speaker's picture of Brendon Gallacher concentrates on what he does and on his family. She never says anything about his imagined appearance except that he has 'big holes in his trousers'. This is because the Brendon Gallacher inside her head needs to be separated from the reality of the toy on which his imagined life is based.

The picture she invents is a romantic and slightly dangerous one. The father isn't merely a burglar; he is a cat burglar, suggesting he is delicate, sensitive and skilful. The family might be poor and the mother might have seven boys and a drink problem but there is a nobility about Brendon, who has a sense of responsibility and duty. He intends to support his mother and take her on holiday. He is protective towards the speaker and holds her hand by the river. She is questioned about him twice. The first time she can deflect the question. The second time it is impossible. Her elaborate fantasy is destroyed suddenly by the intrusion of one basic factual detail, innocently and carelessly offered.

The fantasy cannot be properly recreated now. The speaker gave him life but he is nothing more than an imaginary friend. So he dies. The toy on which the fantasy was based is still there, but the illusion has been destroyed. He was 'flat out on my bedroom floor'.

Examiner's tip: Writing about fragile dreams

Brendon Gallacher is an imaginary friend. The increasingly complex illusion is based initially upon one of the speaker's toys. We know this from the last verse.

She still has the toy, but not the story she so carefully created. When that fantasy dies, so does an important part of her childhood. The theme of the poem is the loss of such innocence. The investment she has made in his identity is wiped away 'after we'd been friends for two years'. The illusion shatters when we hear someone else's voice in the poem, expressing a fact that intrudes into the speaker's fantasy world. Brendon Gallacher is an innocent imaginative dream destroyed by casual reality.

There is longing and regret in the last verse, revealed in the introduction of the expression 'Oh'. It is a perfect expression of her sense of loss. This is also the only time she uses his Christian name alone: 'Oh Brendon. Oh my Brendon Gallacher.'

He has represented the themes of love, devotion, loyalty, tenderness and responsibility and, at the end of the poem, death. The speaker grieves for him.

KEY QUOTE

'She says there are no Gallachers at 24 Novar.'

CHECKPOINT 1

Name another poem which contains a reference to a cat.

COMPARE THIS POEM WITH...

'Ozymandias' also explores the difference between illusion and reality.

'Casehistory: Alison (head injury)' has a similar sense of loss.

'Singh Song!' uses details from domestic life.

U. A. Fanthorpe: 'Casehistory: Alison (head injury)'

SUMMARY

❶ The poet presents the voice of Alison who reflects on how her life has changed.

❷ She has suffered an unexplained head injury that has affected her both mentally and physically.

❸ She looks at a photograph of herself as a young girl.

❹ The photograph seems to be a picture of a completely different person.

❺ Alison knows that the girl in the photograph has no idea what her future will bring. All the potential that is evident in the picture will come to nothing.

EXAMINER'S TIP

Be aware of the craftsmanship of the poet. Some of the poets here adopted a particular form and expressed their thoughts through that shape.

WHAT IS SPECIAL ABOUT THIS POEM?

A The poem gives us a **clear picture** of Alison's **thoughts**.

B The **photograph** provides a **powerful image** around which the key ideas are constructed.

C The theme of **lost potential** might make us reflect on our **identity** and **future**.

D The **idea of death** is at the heart of the poem.

E It uses **contrasts** extremely effectively.

LOST POTENTIAL

KEY QUOTE

'My husband's wife, my mother's only daughter.'

Through the voice of Alison, U. A. Fanthorpe presents a clear picture of the girl in the photograph. She had been confident. She had dealt with the death of her father and, whilst she still grieved for him, she could still smile. She had moved on from that death in a way that she cannot move on from her own injury. The consequences of it haunt her. This is very clearly expressed in the first verse, where she refers to herself as a separate person.

GRADE BOOSTER

Plan your responses carefully. Don't rush into your answers. Signpost the way for yourself by writing a plan. This will ensure that you can move successfully between poems as you write.

The connection between herself then and now has been broken. The girl in the photograph doesn't exist anymore. Alison has lost all knowledge of the memories and thoughts that the earlier Alison possessed. Alison wants 'consistency', to be like the girl in the picture. Then her face was 'broken / By nothing sharper than smiles'. Her body has now been broken in a much more serious way. What happened to her was also a death but one which she has found harder to deal with than the death of her father.

The photograph is full of innocence. However, her hopes and dreams were destroyed. She had her A-levels, 'her job with a future.' But in reality her life would be shaped by the unexpected head injury. That injury, not the photograph, would prove to be the defining moment in her life.

The photograph acts symbolically. It connects Alison with what she once was, because she has become an entirely different person.

CAREFUL CONSTRUCTION

Look at the title. It is a very important part of the poem. It gives you information that doesn't appear elsewhere. That is where you find out that this is about a 'head injury'. Think also about the word 'Casehistory', which makes the poem sound as if it was taken from medical records. The word 'history' is **ironic** since Alison has few clear details about her own past.

The poem has a simple structure in verses of three lines and it has the **rhythm** of ordinary speech with only two verses not ending in a full stop. The word 'I' is repeated to separate the voice of Alison from the photograph of Alison, who is referred to in the third person as 'she'. The poet uses these words to contrast past and present.

The poem is first person narration, a dramatic **monologue** such as 'My Last Duchess' by Robert Browning. We have direct access to Alison's thoughts as she looks at the photograph. It is as if she is looking at a stranger. The knee that once had style and poise 'like a Degas dancer's' now 'lugs' her. In the photograph she was trapped in 'comforting fat'. Today she is trapped in a clumsy body.

The poet shows Alison's daily struggle to remember. She can no longer remember why she might have been smiling in the old photograph. The poem gives an insight into her mental processes and the difficulties she faces. The sentences she uses are short and uncomplicated as if this is all she can manage.

EXAMINER'S TIP: WRITING ABOUT A POET'S TECHNIQUE – CONTRASTS

Think about the way Fanthorpe uses contrasts to make clear the differences between what Alison was once like and what she is like now. Because we hear these things in Alison's own voice, it makes details more immediate and moving. There is a deliberate contrast between two different deaths.

It doesn't matter how clever you are, it is impossible to know what will happen in the future. Even though her brain does not work as well as it did when she was younger, Alison now has the benefit of hindsight and the end of the poem is a chilling reminder of her lost potential.

KEY QUOTE

'I am her future. A bright girl she was.'

COMPARE THIS POEM WITH...

'My Last Duchess' is another example of a monologue in which a person speaks to us directly.

'The Clown Punk' is a similar **character** who has been frozen in time.

'On a Portrait of a Dead Man' also deals with a cruel loss.

'The Ruined Maid' uses the idea of contrasts in a similarly effective way.

CHECKPOINT 2

Name a poem which also features a child's reaction to an unconventional person.

DID YOU KNOW

Punk is a derogatory term with a long history. Shakespeare used it and it eventually became part of the slang used by prisoners to describe younger inmates.

KEY QUOTE

'Slathers his daft mush on the windscreen'

COMPARE THIS POEM WITH...

'Give' deals with someone on the fringes of society.

'The Hunch-back in the Park' also shows children reacting with fear of an unusual stranger.

'Casehistory: Alison (head injury)' is about someone else who is trapped in the past.

Simon Armitage: 'The Clown Punk'

SUMMARY

❶ On his way home the poet occasionally sees the clown punk.

❷ He is dressed in an untidy way.

❸ He is covered in tattoos.

❹ He washes windscreens and frightens children.

❺ The poet imagines him in thirty years' time.

WHAT IS SPECIAL ABOUT THIS POEM?

A The imagery and vocabulary used paint a **vivid picture** of the clown punk.

B The poet makes us **reflect** on the nature of the punk's **rebellion**.

C The poem shows us that the clown punk has made **unwise decisions**.

D The theme explores how what was intended to be intimidating will become comic.

THE POET'S ATTITUDE TO THE PUNK

The poet explores the idea that you cannot maintain a rebellious attitude which is indicated in nothing more than indelible marks on the skin. The punk's tattoos give him an identity from which he can never escape. He cannot turn the clock back and remove either the tattoos or the effect that they have upon others. He has been frozen in time. There is no real sympathy in this poem for the clown punk. He is presented as a tiresome irrelevant figure.

UNWISE DECISIONS

Armitage implies that the clown punk is an unwelcome presence, performing a trivial unimportant task. He can reject normal social values but he still needs other people with cars who might be prepared to pay him. Armitage indicates that rain cleans windscreens just as effectively and more simply.

EXAMINER'S TIP: WRITING ABOUT IMAGERY AND VOCABULARY

Armitage's use of imagery is highly effective because it gives you a real impression of how the clown punk appears, through the use of a vivid initial simile. He is 'like a basket of washing that got up and walked' which captures perfectly his untidy clothes. The poem is very visual and the pictures created indicate that any threat he presents is only skin deep.

The use of the word 'shonky', which means dirty and derelict, invites the reader to connect the clown punk with his environment. However, a clown dresses in untidy baggy clothes for comic effect. It is a disguise. The punk can never remove his disguise.

For the moment his tattoos frighten the children who 'wince and scream', but in the future the tattoos will be 'sad'. As his body and skin changes with age, the marks on him will become comic rather than threatening.

Simon Armitage: 'Give'

SUMMARY

① A homeless person speaks to us directly.

② They are deliberately intruding on our lives.

③ They will do whatever they need to do for money.

④ They do not want anything unusual or grand, just small change.

⑤ They beg for understanding.

WHAT IS SPECIAL ABOUT THIS POEM?

A Armitage creates a powerful atmosphere of **desperation**.

B We hear an **insistent voice** from one side of a meeting or confrontation.

C The poem cleverly brings together two **separate worlds**.

D The poet creates his effects through carefully selected **vocabulary**.

E There are significant links with the details of the **Christmas story**.

ATMOSPHERE

It is clear that the appearance of the homeless person is an unwelcome intrusion. They have chosen to 'make a scene' in a particular place. This deliberate selection is emphasised by the repetition of the word 'chosen'. The use of the word 'dear' gives the poem an uncomfortable and threatening atmosphere. Simon Armitage adopts the persona of a homeless person. The voice makes us feel guilty and uncomfortable. The sentences are short and the words represent ordinary everyday language, yet underpinned by desperation, as seen in the third verse.

THE THEME OF CHRISTMAS

The associations with Christmas begin with the word 'stars' which suggests the Three Wise men. This reference is expanded with the introduction of frankincense and myrrh. What is missing is a reference to the third gift, gold. All he wants is merely 'change'. The idea of small coins links to the concept of changing attitudes. He is on his knees, just as the Three Wise Men knelt before Jesus. He too was homeless.

EXAMINER'S TIP: WRITING ABOUT VOCABULARY

Simon Armitage uses simple everyday words to construct the poem and yet achieves considerable depth of meaning. Look for example at the title. Is this a request? Or an instruction? In the context of this poem it is both. And what should we 'give'? Sympathy and understanding? Money?

The key word in the poem comes at the end of the third verse. It is 'change'. Is this small unwanted coins that are usually given to those who beg? Or is it a change in attitude that stops people becoming homeless?

In the final verse the homeless person is 'on my knees'. Is this a plea, kneeling down before the reader? Or is it a metaphorical reference to their exhaustion and social condition? The last sentence of the poem, which uses the verb 'beg', also has a double meaning. Is it a request for money? Understanding?

KEY QUOTE

'Of all the door-ways in the world to choose to sleep, I've chosen yours.'

COMPARE THIS POEM WITH...

'The Horse Whisperer' is another example of an outsider who is rejected by society.

'The Ruined Maid' also explores the things people are prepared to do to survive.

'Checking Out Me History' is another poem which calls for a change in attitudes.

John Agard: 'Checking Out Me History'

SUMMARY

① The poet tells us that the history of his people has been hidden.

② It seems that his heritage has been deliberately excluded and ignored.

③ This hidden history has within it figures who are far more significant than some of those who are included in European history.

④ He refers to three specific figures from black history who are neglected in spite of their achievements.

⑤ The poet argues that it is time to break free from the political control that has tried to hide his heritage.

WHAT IS SPECIAL ABOUT THIS POEM?

A John Agard uses an **identifiable** and **distinctive voice** that reflects his **culture** and **background**.

B The poem is very carefully and effectively **constructed**.

C The poet makes us question our own **assumptions** about 'British history' that have made us disregard the history of his people.

D He argues that without a proper **history** a people have no proper **identity**.

E John Agard expresses his **frustration** at this neglect and his **determination** that it will not continue.

VOICE AND CONSTRUCTION

The first word of the poem is really significant. It has prominence because it is part of a very short line and establishes an accusatory tone that runs through the poem. 'Dem' try to control him through what they will let him know.

Their significance is emphasised in the repetition of 'dem' in the first three lines and then throughout the rest of the poem. These people are using their version of history as an act of control.

Agard uses repetition to give the poem a shape. You can see this in the last verse, where he compresses the first three lines of the poem into two lines. By the end of the poem what 'dem tell me' is less important because he has decided to reclaim his heritage.

The use of accent and **dialect** throughout emphasises that Agard is the representative voice for a people. He implies that just as his past is to be respected, so is his language and speech patterns. Agard also uses **rhyme** and the repetition of sound to set verses apart. Look for example at the verse about Nelson and Waterloo and the following verse about Florence Nightingale. These have conventional, though different, rhyming patterns. In fact, he mocks some of the childish things he has been taught in the child-like **rhymes** he uses in the verse about 'de cow who jump over de moon'. These are Anglocentric (English-focused) stories. They do not reflect his own Caribbean childhood.

KEY QUOTE

'Blind me to me own identity'

 **DID YOU KNOW**

Toussaint L'Overture was the leader of a revolution by slaves who drove Napoleon's army out of Haiti in the West Indies in the late 18th century.

Nanny de Maroon led her people, the Maroons, in the Windward Islands during the battles against British colonial forces between 1720 and 1739.

The verses about the three figures Agard identifies are very different. They are made up of short lines which give these verses a prominence and power. In each case the person – Toussaint, Nanny and Mary Seacole (see below) – is referred to in the previous verse. He then gives them a verse of their own and shows them as heroic figures who represent the great achievements of Caribbean culture. These verses contain poetic devices such as metaphors that are not found elsewhere.

FRUSTRATION

John Agard is convinced that this neglect should be ended. He has lived too long without proper respect being offered to his heritage. He has not been taught about those who fought for the liberation of their people. He has been enslaved to English culture and taught nursery rhymes such as Old King Cole, rather than the story of those who struggled against oppression.

Knowledge is control. If you can control the knowledge that people have of their own heritage, you can control them. What Agard is saying is that they should fight against this. He uses the example of Mary Seacole who defied the British to go to the Crimea as his own act of defiance and as the inspiration for his determination to check out his own history.

EXAMINER'S TIP: WRITING ABOUT JOHN AGARD'S VIEW OF HISTORY

John Agard talks about the European version of history he has been taught, where significant people from black history are ignored. Toussaint L'Overture and Nanny de Maroon who fought for freedom are excluded. He refers to colonial history in South Africa and America and reminds us that the historical record was written by Europeans, not by the native people. How for example can Columbus be said to have discovered America when the Caribs and the Arawacks were already there?

The use of Mary Seacole as an example is significant. She travelled across the world to help wounded soldiers in the Crimean War. It was a European war that had nothing to do with her and yet she acted out of a concern for other people. So why should the story of 'a healing star / among the wounded' be suppressed? Agard implies that it is merely because she came from Jamaica.

EXAMINER'S TIP

Develop your understanding by design. Make spider diagrams or mind maps. These might help you in drawing up connections between the poems.

KEY QUOTE

'But now I checking out me own history I carving out me identity'

COMPARE THIS POEM WITH...

'**Casehistory: Alison (Head injury)**' is an example of what happens when someone loses contact with their own history.

'**The Horse Whisperer**' shows a community which is determined to deny its history rather than reclaim it.

'**Singh Song!**' is an example of how the cultural landscape of Britain is expanding.

'**Brendon Gallacher**' uses the repetition of words and phrases in a similarly effective way.

Dorothy Molloy: 'Les Grands Seigneurs'

SUMMARY

1. The female speaker recalls how she enjoyed the presence of men.

2. They were the most important part of her life.

3. She enjoyed the influence she had over them.

4. Her status changed when she married.

5. She was obliged to obey her husband.

GRADE BOOSTER

There isn't much to be gained by just mentioning a technique or device. You must always comment on the effect that it has in order to achieve the higher grades.

WHAT IS SPECIAL ABOUT THIS POEM?

A The poem has a very **distinctive voice** which reflects on her experience.

B Dorothy Molloy uses a complex range of **metaphors** to explore her viewpoint about the relationship between men and women.

C The **title** adds significantly to our understanding of the poem.

D The **structure** used by the poet reflects her changing relationship with men.

E The poem offers us **surprising insights** into how **circumstances** change us as people.

TITLE

The title is very interesting. 'Les Grands Seigneurs' is French and means 'the great lords'. Initially it is an **ironic** title as we can see in the first three verses. It suggests that the men are patronising and foolish. They might think they are the masters but in these verses the speaker is in control. The title also establishes the **atmosphere** of a medieval world which is sustained in the use of images such as castles, damsels, courtly love and troubadours. In this romantic world the men defer to her and protect her. She is 'the peach', a woman of the highest quality, the very best.

EXAMINER'S TIP

A good plan helps you organise complex material in an examination.

MEN

In the presence of men the speaker sheltered from reality. This is why they are described like a castle. Through them she experienced a whole range of emotions.

She was able to reflect on what they did. Like birds they were desperate to make themselves attractive to find a mate. They were entertaining and she enjoyed their attention. They amused her with their high opinions of themselves. They filled every part of her world – the air (the references to birds), the water (the references to the sea) and the earth (the horses and the monkeys).

The use of the possessive pronoun 'my' emphasises her feeling that she was in control. She behaved as if she was their queen. As such she was untouchable.

Her status changed instantly the moment she married, 'yes, overnight'. Instead of a person in control, she changes into a wife. The impact of this is emphasised by the poet's introduction of the only **rhyme** in the poem – 'bedded' and 'wedded'. The language in this verse represents a return to reality. It is much more straightforward and abandons the rich **imagery** of the rest of the poem.

What the verse makes clear is that everything previously had been a game. Her husband knew that. His power was much simpler and more easily displayed. He 'called my bluff' and she had to obey. An illusion is shattered. Reality replaces romance.

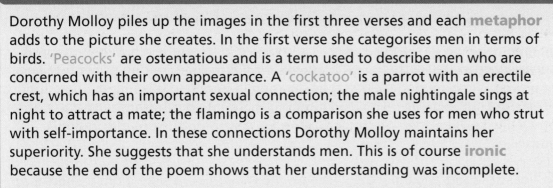

EXAMINER'S TIP: WRITING ABOUT DOROTHY MOLLOY'S USE OF METAPHOR

Dorothy Molloy piles up the images in the first three verses and each **metaphor** adds to the picture she creates. In the first verse she categorises men in terms of birds. 'Peacocks' are ostentatious and is a term used to describe men who are concerned with their own appearance. A 'cockatoo' is a parrot with an erectile crest, which has an important sexual connection; the male nightingale sings at night to attract a mate; the flamingo is a comparison she uses for men who strut with self-importance. In these connections Dorothy Molloy maintains her superiority. She suggests that she understands men. This is of course **ironic** because the end of the poem shows that her understanding was incomplete.

In the second verse she turns to the sea for her material. Dolphins often accompany a ship, just as men accompany her, for she refers to herself as a ship in the second line where she writes about 'ballast in my hold'. It is also a name for a fish design in heraldry which maintains the medieval atmosphere she has created through the title and the castle imagery. In this verse she sees the men performing to order, like seals or monkeys. She also sees them as faintly ridiculous by using the metaphor 'rocking-horses / prancing down the promenade'.

She stays out of their reach as a queen. It was a controlled romantic environment where she teased the men with her innocence and her sexuality. The peach has sexual **connotations** in many cultures, including French, since it is seen to represent female genitalia.

Everything changes in the last verse. The poet describes how her husband takes control away from her merely by clicking his fingers. She may have had the ability to maintain control over men previouslyt, but now she is 'a bit of fluff'. The game has ended and her power has gone.

KEY QUOTE

'...The best and worst of times were men'

KEY QUOTE

'I was their queen. I sat enthroned before them'

COMPARE THIS POEM WITH...

'**Brendon Gallacher**' also deals with the end of a controlled relationship.

'**The Ruined Maid**' is about a woman whose life is defined by her relationship with men.

'**Singh Song!**' is also about relationships.

Carol Ann Duffy: 'Medusa'

SUMMARY

1 Medusa describes how she has changed and become a monstrous creature.

2 Her happiness and optimism have been replaced by anger and hatred because she has been betrayed by a man.

3 She is full of destructive emotions.

4 Medusa realises that she has developed dangerous and magical powers.

5 She wants to turn her lover to stone in an act of revenge.

WHAT IS SPECIAL ABOUT THIS POEM?

A Carol Ann Duffy interweaves the **myth** of Medusa with the **emotions** of a jealous or wronged woman.

B The poem explores the idea of **transformation**.

C She uses very **powerful language** to emphasise the **changes** that have taken place in Medusa.

D Carol Ann Duffy uses **simple words** and **sentence structures** in a highly effective way.

E The **final line** of the poem provides a **powerful ending** that draws upon the myth of Medusa in a memorable way.

SIMPLE WORDS AND STRUCTURES

The great triumph of the poem is that it works on different levels. When you look at it as a picture of the mythological Medusa, it is a literal description of her fate and her power. When you regard it as a poem about a wronged woman, the descriptions become metaphorical and give an intense insight into her feelings and those of any betrayed wife or partner. All this is achieved in a simple structure and in simple vocabulary.

The lines are short and emphatic, because the thoughts are simple ones. There is no complication in what she thinks. There is no doubt in her mind. She wants revenge. The question and its answer which span verses two and three have simple emotive power by linking love with terror.

Throughout the poem she uses words that have negative or unpleasant meanings. Words such as 'spat', 'soured', 'stank' and 'spewed' all begin with the same sound (**assonance**), which recalls the hissing of the snakes on her head. The words remind us of unpleasant processes of a human body that she wants to turn to stone. The animals that she looks at increase gradually in size. Any pleasure in bees or birds or cats disappears. They are moving and active. They make sounds such as 'buzzing', 'singing' and 'snuffling'. But the life is suddenly drawn out of them. The words she chooses emphasise how they have been changed into something colourless, silent and inanimate – 'pebble', 'gravel' and 'boulder'.

There is one important **rhyme** at the very heart of the poem. It is in the third verse and links together 'own' and 'stone', which confirms her desire to possess the man. The only way she can do this is to turn him into lifeless stone.

THE END OF THE POEM

The final verse tells us more about the man who has betrayed her. He has a 'shield for a heart' that protects him from real commitment. She now knows that he never let her know his real feelings.

The repetition of 'your girls' has considerable power because of the use of the possessive 'your' and suggests how this Medusa has been betrayed. She looks back at what she once was and what he has destroyed.

The final line is a complete sentence: 'Look at me now.' The sentence is asking him to face up to his responsibilities. It is a command because she knows that she has power as a result of the emotions that have been released. But it also refers to the myth of Medusa. 'Look at me now' and be turned to stone.

EXAMINER'S TIP: WRITING ABOUT TRANSFORMATION IN 'MEDUSA'

Duffy establishes a different context to the myth in the very first line. A suspicion suddenly runs out of control and becomes 'jealousy'. The transformation of her beautiful hair into 'filthy' snakes is just a physical manifestation of the turmoil inside her head. Her thoughts are evil. Like Medusa she was ready for love but that love has been transformed into jealousy. She may have been beautiful once but now she has been physically transformed by that same jealousy. Her breath smells, her lungs have become 'grey bags' and her mouth 'foul' and 'yellow'.

The **theme** of the poem is that love is no longer positive or life enhancing. It has been transformed into something that inspires terror.

She regarded her man as perfect but she is worried that she will lose him. The only way she can keep him, to possess him, is to turn him into stone.

The emotions that have been unleashed have the power to destroy. They can suck the colour and the life out of living things and turn them into stone. The transformation of the animals is merely a rehearsal for the transformation of a man. This will be an act both of revenge and of control. When she turns him to stone, he can never leave.

All this is a consequence of the transformation of love. What was once beautiful is now destructive.

Robert Browning: 'My Last Duchess'

SUMMARY

❶ During a pause in arranging a new bride, the duke who narrates the poem shows an envoy a picture of his previous wife.

❷ The picture was very skilfully painted by Fra Pandolf.

❸ The duke was not happy with the way his wife behaved.

❹ He tells the envoy that he arranged for her to be silenced.

❺ They return downstairs to resume their discussions.

> **KEY QUOTE**
>
> '…This grew: I gave commands; Then all smiles stopped together.'

WHAT IS SPECIAL ABOUT THIS POEM?

A It is a poem of outstanding **technique** and **craftsmanship**.

B Browning uses a **dialogue** to reveal in a dramatic way what the duke has done.

C We are given a **complex** and **detailed** picture of the duke.

D The poet **presents** the duchess as a **victim**.

E Browning uses **inference** and **implication** to create a sense of **foreboding** for the next duchess.

TECHNIQUE

This is one of the great English poems. Robert Browning's achievement in this poem is that he reveals so many possibilities by allowing a **character** to speak for himself in a **monologue**. We are in the position of the envoy listening to the duke, which makes the emotional impact of his words even greater. The power of the poem comes from this directness. It is written in rhyming **couplets** but it has the energy of ordinary speech. His use of **enjambment** means that the **rhymes** rarely fall at the end of a sentence and we thus listen to what sounds like a real conversation. He balances long sentences with short ones to great effect.

The duke speaks in a conversational tone that contrasts with the horror of what he has done. To him, his actions appear absolutely acceptable. His wife was an object and when he became dissatisfied, he disposed of her. Now she is a picture she is much easier to control.

His vocabulary is also significant. Notice that her behaviour does not upset him or irritate him. It 'disgusts' him. He tells the envoy that the count's 'fair daughter's self … is my object.' We cannot believe him, particularly as Browning places this comment immediately after a reference to the dowry. The word 'object' is revealing. He reduced his first wife to an object. In describing an imagined conversation, he refers to 'the faint / Half-flush that dies along her throat'. These are chilling words. Now that Browning has established his character, we can see that this is a reference to either a cut throat or to strangulation.

> **CHECKPOINT 4**
>
> Name another poem which refers to a work of art.

>  **DID YOU KNOW**
>
> A dowry was a gift given by the bride's family in an arranged marriage. It could be money, jewels or property. The bigger the dowry, the more important the husband.

THE DUCHESS

The presentation of the duchess's character is mediated through the duke's words, but we learn that she took pleasure in everything around her. For the duke this devalued his family. He regarded her as too free spirited. So he replaced her with a painting that can be admired and which will never change. His wife is now as he prefers her – a possession.

Many possibilities emerge as we piece together the story. Perhaps she was a lively interesting woman, loved by her servants as a breath of fresh air in the stifling self-important formality of the court. Perhaps the duke believed her enjoyment of life was flirtatious; perhaps he feared she was unfaithful. It is a sign of Browning's considerable skill that he can imply this whilst only using the duke's own words.

EXAMINER'S TIP: WRITING ABOUT THE DUKE

The hesitations Browning introduces into his speech – 'how shall I say?', 'I know not how' – give him an air of bewilderment. These hesitations also make him seem real, as if he is engaged in a conversation with both the envoy and the reader. He wants us to see him as a reasonable man of taste and refinement. He tries to establish himself as a discerning art lover, speaking with admiration of the work of Fra Pandolf. He admires the technique and skill and seems more proud of the picture than he ever was of the real woman.

He is prepared to talk about what he has done as if it was the most natural thing to do. Browning shows that the duke expects everyone to see the world as he does. He removed the duchess because she was wrong. It was not his responsibility to correct her, 'I choose / Never to stoop.' The duke was far too proud for this. Why does he tell the envoy these things? Is it a subtle warning about how he expects any new wife to behave? Like Neptune, the sea god, he will have to tame her and he expects to succeed.

He is confident that the count, whose daughter he now wishes to marry, will offer him a suitable dowry. This is emphasised as they go down stairs, when he refers to another piece of artwork. 'Notice Neptune … Taming a sea horse'. It is a possession to be proud of, to be valued. There is no sense of horror of what he has said to the envoy as he returns to where he started, talking of craftsmanship and ownership.

? **DID YOU KNOW**

The poem was published in 1842. The character of the duke in the poem is based on the character of Alfonso II, the Duke of Ferrara (1533–98). His young wife died in mysterious circumstances in April 1561 when she was 17.

KEY QUOTE

'…She thanked men, – good! But thanked Somehow – I know not how – as if she ranked My gift of a nine-hundred-years-old name With anybody's gift.'

COMPARE THIS POEM WITH…

'The River God' also shows a character who exercises absolute power.

'Les Grands Seigneurs' is also about a woman subjugated by a man.

'Medusa' is an examination of irrational behaviour.

There are numerous other mono-logues in this cluster such as **'Casehistory: Alison (head injury)'**.

Andrew Forster: 'The Horse Whisperer'

SUMMARY

① The horse whisperer would respond to requests to calm anxious horses.

② He used a variety of charms and objects to treat them.

③ The horses were suddenly replaced by tractors.

④ When the horse whisperer was driven away he left a curse behind him.

⑤ He misses the power and the majesty of the horses.

KEY QUOTE

'I was the life-blood no longer.'

KEY CONNECTIONS

The Horse Whisperer is also the name of a film released in 1995 starring Robert Redford. It was based on a novel by Nicholas Evans about a trainer with an uncanny understanding of horses.

WHAT IS SPECIAL ABOUT THIS POEM?

A Andrew Forster examines the effects of the **passage of time** through an interesting **structure**.

B The **power** of **horses** is evoked with subtle and imaginative imagery.

C References to charms and **superstition** reveal a world changed by **modern life**.

D The reader is invited to **empathise** with a man who has unusual powers.

E The theme of the poem is that his powers eventually lead to his **rejection**.

UNUSUAL POWERS

The horse whisperer has a clear understanding of his own skill. You can see the contrast between the title, which gives prominence to the word 'Whisperer' and the owners who 'shouted'. He can subdue powerful animals with 'shimmering muscles' by using charms such as 'spongy tissue' and 'frog's wishbone'.

He has the ability to calm the fear of the humans and the horses quietly. He can bring two different animals together to work in harmony. He understands the strength and power of the horses. He uses verbs which emphasise movement like 'traced circles' and 'reared'. He controls them through his influence, not his strength.

When the community turns against him, he leaves a curse above the stable door. Notice the rhyme that links 'door' and 'more', giving the curse prominence.

DRIVEN AWAY

His ancient skills made others frightened of him. When they felt they didn't need him any more, they turned against him.

Technology drives away the old skills and religion is used to condemn 'this legacy of whisperers'. He is now regarded as a 'demon'. By leaving the 'hex above the stable door', he confirms what they now think about him.

COMPARE THIS POEM WITH...

'The River God' deals with a character out of step with the modern world.

In **'Brendon Gallacher'** a happy time is also destroyed in an instant.

'On a Portrait of a Deaf Man' also confronts the influence of conventional religion.

EXAMINER'S TIP: WRITING ABOUT TIME

Each verse gets progressively shorter, reflecting the decline in his influence. He has more to say about the past when he was important to others but he is separated by the passage of time from his achievements. Now all he has are memories. The shortening of the verses gives a sense of the speed at which time passes. The horse whisperer can never return to a time when he was valued and respected.

Dylan Thomas: 'The Hunchback in the Park'

SUMMARY

1. A lonely and poor hunchback spends his days in the park.
2. Boys tease him when they play.
3. Both the boys and the hunchback invent rich fantasies whilst they are there.
4. In the evening they all leave their fantasies behind in the park.
5. The hunchback returns alone to his poor home.

WHAT IS SPECIAL ABOUT THIS POEM?

A The poet uses imagery from the natural world very effectively.

B A child's view of the world is presented in an interesting way.

C The sadness at the heart of the poem is vividly portrayed.

D The park is presented as a place of freedom and dreams.

E The poem contrasts the dreams of the hunchback with the imaginary world of the boys in a moving way.

A CHILD'S VIEW

Dylan Thomas presents a solitary and static figure who contrasts with truant boys who are always in motion. Their imaginations transform the park into a place of adventure and daring, where 'tigers jumped out of their eyes'. They make fun of the hunchback and believe that he lives in a kennel. They tease him and play tricks. They celebrate their freedom and energy noisily. The hunchback is more absorbed in his thoughts. Where the boys find freedom in their games, he finds freedom within himself.

THE PARK

The park is a fantasy world where the hunchback and the boys can recreate their dreams and escape from themselves. The hunchback creates a woman. In his mind he turns his twisted body into something perfect and beautiful. She has no life without him. He can only create her when the boys disappear into their own imaginative world. The real things that happened to the hunchback in the day he takes home as memories – 'the birds' and the 'wild boys' – but the dream stays behind. The 'kennel in the dark' repeats the suggestion of death from the first verse ('The Sunday sombre bell') and in this way Thomas increases our sympathy for the hunchback.

EXAMINER'S TIP: WRITING ABOUT STRUCTURE

The poem has strong rhymes and three full stops which divide it into three sections. The first introduces the poem. The next two verses deal with the boys. The last section reveals the dream that brings the hunchback back to the park.

The first and last verses are framed by the same rhyme which link 'park' and 'dark'. The rhyme scheme in the middle section represents the boys running around. In the first two verses of the last section there are no rhymes, which suits the reflective nature of the hunchback. The vocabulary is rich with references to the natural world.

CHECKPOINT 5

Identify another poem which contains a reference to trees.

KEY QUOTE

'Laughing when he shook his paper Hunchbacked in mockery'

COMPARE THIS POEM WITH...

'Give' is another example of a poem about a disadvantaged person.

In 'The Clown Punk' children also come into contact with someone who is an outsider.

'The River God' is also about an old man who wants companionship but is forever lonely.

Daljit Nagra: 'Singh Song!'

SUMMARY

EXAMINER'S TIP

Consider how the characters in these poems sometimes stand outside accepted social values.

① Singh the shopkeeper has recently married.

② He would rather spend time with his wife than carry out his duties.

③ His wife has unconventional attitudes.

④ He does not serve the needs of his community as they expect because he prefers to follow his heart.

⑤ When the shop is closed, Singh and his wife sit together in the darkness and he tells her how much he loves her.

WHAT IS SPECIAL ABOUT THIS POEM?

A The **voice** and the **community** that the poem represents are very carefully depicted.

B The poem is based upon the **contrast** between expectations and reality.

C We have a **convincing** picture of Singh, the love sick and naïve shopkeeper.

D We see his wife **through Singh's words** – and we see things that he does not.

E The poet engages us with a **compelling** and **unconventional** love story.

VOICE AND CULTURE

The language of the poem is very distinctive, coming from the heart of the community it represents. Nagra captures the rhythm of everyday speech very convincingly. There is little punctuation to interrupt the flow of Singh's voice. The details Nagra selects reflect the commodities in the shop – chapatti, chutney, limes, bananas, bread, milk, chocolate – where the poem takes place.

Another voice which Nagra introduces is the traditional Indian community which comments on Singh's capabilities as a shopkeeper, like a chorus in a Bollywood film. They intrude into his world twice and remind him of his failures. All they want is a clean shop where the lemons are not like limes. They represent the conventional life from which the wife wants to escape.

KEY QUOTE

'di tings yoo hav on offer yoo hav never got in stock in di worst Indian shop on di whole Indian road –'

The wife speaks on two occasions to ask questions about how much her husband loves her, as if she needs reassurance. It is significant that Singh and his wife stare away from the shop and the community in the evening. Nagra explores the meeting of three cultures – a traditional Indian culture, Western culture and a modern Indian culture which doesn't seem to belong to either and which is represented by the wife. The poet structures the verses in different shapes to reflect the different voices we hear. The voice of the customers holds it together. There is also repetition of 'my bride' in the middle of the poem which makes clear Singh's devotion. Nothing is more important to him than their love. At the end of the poem their peaceful dialogue appears like a love duet in a film. A Singh song perhaps.

THE CHARACTER OF SINGH

Singh is not driven like his father, who has a number of shops. Singh can barely run one. He neglects his duties and locks up the shop rather than cleaning it, so that he can go upstairs to make love to his wife. When he is downstairs, he listens to her constantly using the computer. He accepts the fact that girls steal sweets from the shop. Because of her, he looks outside his traditional community, ignoring its needs and expectations. She has changed his outlook completely. He accepts without question the disrespect she offers to his family.

EXAMINER'S TIP: WRITING ABOUT HOW SINGH'S WIFE IS PRESENTED

The poem brings together a range of emotions and creates the voice of a **narrator** as a real person, in love with a complex woman. She is unpredictable and subversive. Singh accepts what she does without question. She is drawing him away from his heritage.

She is not a dutiful daughter-in-law and her characterisation develops from her actions. She swears at his mother and makes fun of his father. This suggests that a traditional Indian lifestyle has no attraction for her. She seems to be dangerous with 'tiny eyes ov a gun'. She has not adapted to his way of life. She takes no part in the business, only appearing down stairs once the shop is closed. She spends her time upstairs wearing high heels and using the internet. The heels are a **symbol** of her desire to be elsewhere for they are not the shoes for work. It is her husband who dresses for work in his 'pinnie'. She seems disengaged from the shop. Her dress is unconventional and she has more in common with the girls who come in to steal the sweets.

This adds to the sense that she is restless and discontented. In the evening she looks at the moon as if she wants to escape from her life. There is a contrast between that image of the moon and half-price chocolate. She wants to hear Singh say how much she is worth. She asks two questions about the value of things. She does not talk of her love for him.

CHECKPOINT 6

Name two other poems which refer to marriage.

KEY QUOTE

'She hav a red crew cut
and she wear a tartan sari
a donkey jacket and some pumps'

COMPARE THIS POEM WITH...

'The Ruined Maid' is a poem about another woman who is dissatisfied with her lifestyle.

'Medusa' deals with different aspects of love.

'Checking Out Me History' also has a distinctive ethnic voice.

'My Last Duchess' is another poem which allows us to see beyond the narrator's words.

Stevie Smith: 'The River God'

SUMMARY

① We hear the voice of a forgotten river god in this poem.

② Although he is old and neglected, he still has the power of life and death, which he enjoys.

③ A woman has drowned and the river god holds on to her body.

④ He wants to wash away her fear.

⑤ She was an ordinary woman who drowned. The river god now possesses her.

CHECKPOINT 7

Which other poem(s) from the cluster contain(s) a reference to water?

WHAT IS SPECIAL ABOUT THIS POEM?

A   Stevie Smith creates a convincing **impression** of the **character** of the river god.

B   He **reveals** himself in his **own words**.

C   The river god is presented as a **mythological** character.

D   The poet varies the **rhyme** and the **rhythm** to emphasise her meaning.

E   The poem examines what lies **beneath** the **surface** of the river and of love.

THE RIVER GOD

Stevie Smith gives the river god an element of self-awareness. He speaks honestly and openly. He is old, untidy and unkempt. The poet may be implying that because we do not believe in river gods anymore, he is old and forgotten. But he still has power when he chooses to use it. He protects the fish but sometimes he turns on the people who bathe in him. Fish belong in the river; people do not.

He makes decisions about life and death. As a god he has no reason to justify anything that he does. His absolute and arbitrary power leads to random cruelty. The use of the word 'can' in line 5 implies that he makes choices about who will live and who will die. He regards people as 'fools'.

He describes death in jaunty language as if it is a game. His voice reveals his enjoyment in the nonsense words he uses, contrasting with the tragedy of death by drowning. He enjoys the suffering of his victims, quite untouched by what he has done to them. As the poet indicates, because he is immortal his understanding of life and death is incomplete.

He shows no compassion. The introduction of a regular rhyme scheme in the central part of the poem emphasises the movement of the water that carries the victims away. He has dragged a woman into his depths for companionship. He feels that she should be grateful, but however hard he tries, he cannot change the expression on her face. The vocabulary of the poem emphasises that he inhabits an alien world where mortals do not belong. As a result, his love is destructive.

DID YOU KNOW

The inspiration for the poem was the River Mimram that runs through north Hertfordshire.

KEY QUOTE

'And they take a long time drowning As I throw them up now and then in the spirit of clowning.'

Myth

In the past, rivers had a significance that they do not have today. They were regarded as living things that brought fertility and life. However, they are also dangerous. The river is an element from which we are excluded. It is another world that we can see but in which we cannot live. It was often believed that rivers had their own god.

Such beliefs have disappeared. The voice of the river god is a reminder of the past but although he is forgotten, he is still dangerous. He can still act in a vengeful way. He takes a life to remind other people of the power he has.

The poem uses the idea that gods will sometimes steal humans to live with them. This river god has selected a woman to be his lover. But he can only do this if he drowns her. But where gods are immortal, humans are not. He does not seem to understand the consequences of death.

He behaves as a god does, without any need to explain or justify what he has done. But he will remain forever alone.

At the heart of the poem there is a question: 'Oh will she stay with me will she stay / This beautiful lady, or will she go away?' No matter what he does, a human will never be able to live in his world.

EXAMINER'S TIP: WRITING ABOUT ASPECTS OF LOVE

The river god likes women. He likes to envelop them and to hide them away. He is fearful that they do not want to stay with him because he knows he is 'an old foul river'. So he does not give them a choice.

His victim may be part of his world now, with the hair on her 'golden sleepy head' resembling waving reeds but he can never wash away the fear that is now on her face. His love does not enhance life; it takes life away.

Her own choices and feelings are not important. He has taken her to his bed for his pleasure, but it is a riverbed where humans cannot live. So he will always be condemned to loneliness. He can inspire fear and bring death but he can never experience love.

KEY CONNECTIONS

The character of Ophelia in Shakespeare's *Hamlet* drowns herself in a river. This was the subject of a famous painting by J. E. Millais in 1851 which you can see in the Tate Gallery in London.

KEY QUOTE

'Oh who would guess what a beautiful white face lies there'

COMPARE THIS POEM WITH...

'The Horse Whisperer' deals with ancient and forgotten powers.

'Medusa' uses myth to examine the possessive and destructive aspects of love.

'Les Grands Seigneurs' explores similar issues about the nature of love.

Thomas Hardy: 'The Ruined Maid'

SUMMARY

1. Two young women meet and talk together. They once lived on the same farm but now they have different lives.
2. Amelia has moved away and is leading a much more comfortable life in the town as a 'ruined' woman.
3. She may now be considered an immoral person because of the lifestyle she leads.
4. Those who stayed behind on the farm continue to live in rural poverty.
5. Amelia indicates that there are advantages to an immoral lifestyle.

WHAT IS SPECIAL ABOUT THIS POEM?

A Two **different** characters are successfully presented.

B The poet uses **dialogue** to present **contrasting** perspectives on town life.

C Life on the farm is presented in a very **negative** way.

D Thomas Hardy does **not condemn** Amelia for the decision she made.

E Amelia **appears** to be happy with the choice she has made.

STRUCTURE

The poem is a fine example of structure. It is based on an unexpected encounter on the street and the resulting dialogue between characters who once knew each other. Hardy puts ideas into a coherent shape using a strict structure within which he creates a revealing picture of two different lifestyles. He does this by allowing the two characters to speak for themselves.

The country girl speaks excitedly at this unexpected meeting. She asks questions in verse one, particularly about her old friend's clothes, and then her excitement takes over. Every other statement is an exclamation. She is perhaps shocked by Amelia but also envious, as we can see in the last verse.

Each of these verses begins with an image of the life Amelia has left behind – her clothes, her language, her skin. The country girl talks about the past in order to provide a contrast with how Amelia is now.

Amelia offers single-line comments until the last verse. Hers are simple, **ironic** answers, almost like punchlines.

The poem has a very musical effect because of the repetition of 'ruined said she' at the end of every verse. This means that the same sounds are reproduced throughout, since the last two lines in each verse always **rhyme** using the same sound. Also notice the parallel between the rhymes in the first and last verses that frame the poem.

Amelia listens to her old friend with tolerance. Indeed she reveals her sense of humour at the end of the third verse when she shows how much her accent has changed when she says 'Some polish is gained with one's ruin'. In the last verse she deliberately returns to the words she used in her previous life perhaps to mock her envious friend – 'You ain't ruined'.

HARDY'S VIEWPOINT

The poet offers no condemnation of Amelia. Indeed he chose her name deliberately. It is derived from the Latin 'melior' which means 'better'. Has she made her life better? It is hard to condemn her when it is presented as the most practical solution.

The question Thomas Hardy asks is who is right? Who is leading the better and the most fulfilled life? Of course there isn't a simple answer. Amelia appears to have benefitted from her decision whereas her friend still lives 'a hag-ridden dream'.

When we look at the title, we can see that there is no indication which one of them is actually ruined. Is it Amelia, who is morally ruined by stepping into prostitution? Or the country girl, who will be physically ruined by overwork and manual labour?

EXAMINER'S TIP: WRITING ABOUT AMELIA 🔓

For Amelia morality is a commodity. The theme of the poem is that she has defied conventional attitudes in exchange for a more comfortable life. She wears 'bracelets', 'gloves' and 'feathers'. Her old friend is envious of the things she has. Amelia has no regrets, but we know little about her emotional life.

Her ruin can be seen to have had a positive effect on her. Amelia was once 'a raw country girl' too, but she escaped rural hardship.

If she is a victim of anything, she is a victim of rural squalor, but then so is the other girl. The difference is that Amelia decided to do something about it. It was a lifestyle that made Amelia so unhappy, but will there at some point be a price to pay perhaps?

Their lives are now entirely separate. This is illustrated in the dialects Hardy employs which emphasise the division between town and country. Amelia has experienced life in the country but her friend has not experienced life in town. She will never have the feathers or the sweeping gown. She will never achieve a delicate face unless she leaves her rural life behind and loses her innocence like Amelia.

Amelia had no economic power, so she sold the only thing she had – herself – for a better life. What is your conclusion about Amelia and the message of the poem?

CHECKPOINT 9

Find another poem which contains a reference to potatoes.

KEY QUOTE

'You ask me to believe You and
I only see decay.'

COMPARE THIS POEM WITH...

In **'Case-history: Alison (head injury)'** a character thinks about a person who is no longer alive.

'Brendon Gallacher' also deals with a bereavement.

'Medusa' is about a person being transformed.

John Betjeman: 'On a Portrait of a Deaf Man'

SUMMARY

❶ The poet remembers his father who has died.

❷ His father continued to enjoy life even after he became deaf.

❸ Betjeman considers the contrast between how his father was when he was alive and how he is now that he is dead.

❹ His body has decayed; only the deafness remains the same.

❺ The death of his father makes the poet question the nature of religious belief.

WHAT IS SPECIAL ABOUT THIS POEM?

A   Betjeman creates a **clear picture** of his father, both alive and dead.

B   Betjeman's **depth of feeling** for his father is shown in the **words** he chooses.

C   Betjeman takes a **sombre** theme and explores it subtly.

D   The **emotions** in the poem move from affection, regret and sorrow to anger.

E   The careful **structure** of the poem means that Betjeman uses rhymes to emphasise the movement from life to death.

BETJEMAN'S FATHER

The poet creates an effective picture of his father who was prosperous and educated, with a wide social network. He enjoyed the different aspects of his life. He liked London and the atmosphere of the 'rain-washed Cornish air'. In death, the things that made him different are no longer relevant. The walks, the friendships, the clothes, the personality don't matter anymore. For Betjeman, in death all that happens is that the body decays.

BETJEMAN'S VOICE

The poet's voice deals with different emotions. There is affection in the way he talks about his father's dress sense. He likes to remember him and the things that he did. But he cannot forget the reality of death. The effects of decay can never be reversed. He identifies parts of the body because he is unable to accept the existence of the soul.

EXAMINER'S TIP: WRITING ABOUT STRUCTURE

Betjeman constructs the poem in verses which contrast life and death. This gives the poem a sense of control which is ironic, for it is impossible to control death. Betjeman rhymes ordinary words with death. In the first verse, when he writes about clothes he uses 'loud' and 'shroud'; later when he writes about sight he links 'wise' and 'eyes'. Significantly, in the last verse the rhyme links 'pray' and 'decay'. The verses move from life to death. The first two lines describe how he was alive. Then Betjeman imagines him now that he is dead.

Each verse deals with different senses. There is sight in the first verse and taste in the second. He liked the 'smell of ploughed-up soil' and the sense of touch features in the reference to shaking hands. Which sense does not feature?

Percy Bysshe Shelley: 'Ozymandias'

SUMMARY

① The **narrator** recalls a conversation with a traveller.

② The traveller spoke of a broken statue he had seen of Ozymandias, an ancient king.

③ The ancient sculptor's skill captured the expression on the king's face.

④ Words remain visible on the pedestal.

⑤ The shattered statue is surrounded by empty desert.

WHAT IS SPECIAL ABOUT THIS POEM?

A   There are **three voices** in the poem – the narrator, the traveller and the king.

B   Shelley gives a **detailed picture** of the statue.

C   The poem is written as a **sonnet**.

D   A short **sentence** defines the nature of **mankind's ambitions**.

E   The poem deals with the nature of **power** and **human pride**.

THE PEDESTAL

The words on the pedestal were originally designed to inspire fear and awe. Now they inspire pity. Everything has been levelled. The words that survive now indicate power over a featureless desert and are therefore **ironic**. If we look for his works there is nothing to see, except 'lone and level sands'.

THE SONNET FORM

The poem is a sonnet written in **iambic pentameter**. The fourteen lines are divided into two parts, the first eight lines are the octave where the power of Ozymandias is established and the sextet shows the emptiness of the words on the pedestal. The two parts have separate **rhyme** patterns.

However, in the octave, line 7 does not rhyme with any other, which makes it stand out. It ends with the words 'lifeless things'. It provides a link to the sextet because it rhymes with line 10, 'Ozymandias, king of kings'. It not only links the two parts of the sonnet, but also shows that this boastful claim no longer has any meaning.

The poem is written in long flowing sentences. The short sentence at the beginning of line 12 has huge impact in comparison. It is the final judgement on his legacy: 'Nothing beside remains'.

EXAMINER'S TIP: WRITING ABOUT THE STATUE

Through the statue of Ozymandias, Shelley explores the **themes** of power and vanity. The statue is a 'colossal wreck' and is a **symbol** of what he means to us today. He means nothing. It isn't just the statue that is ruined. All of Ozymandias's work has become desert. All human vanity will disappear into the sands of time just like his. The passions that the sculptors captured in his expression still remain on the broken stone but ironically the artist's creation has survived longer than any of Ozymandias's achievements. Great art is permanent; political power is temporary.

CHECKPOINT 10

Find another poem which refers to a broken face.

? DID YOU KNOW

Shelley wrote the sonnet in an unofficial competition with his friend Horace Smith to see who could write the best poem about the statue.

KEY QUOTE

'"... Look on my works, ye mighty, and despair!"'

COMPARE THIS POEM WITH...

'Casehistory: Alison (head injury)' is another poem which deals with the difference between the present and the past.

'The Horse Whisperer' shows that achievement can be forgotten.

'My Last Duchess' also has an egotistical arrogant central character.

Progress and revision check

Revision activity

① Which poem shows us a ginger cat which is turned into a house brick? (Write your answers below)

....

② In which poem do two **characters** sit together and look at the 'brightey moon'?

....

③ Which character in a poem is described as a cat burglar?

....

④ In which poem is there a reference to Highgate Hill?

....

⑤ Who describes the ruined statue in 'Ozymandias'?

....

Revision activity

On a piece of paper write down answers to these questions:

● What impression do we form of the **narrator** in 'Give' by Simon Armitage?

Start: *The narrator of 'Give' is a homeless person who deliberately intrudes into our lives. They speak…*

● What part does the mother play in the poem 'Brendon Gallacher' by Jackie Kay?

Start: *Although she doesn't realise it, Jackie Kay's mother plays a crucial part in the poem because…*

GRADE BOOSTER

Answer this longer, practice question about 'Singh Song!' by Daljit Nagra

Q: How does Daljit Nagra show that Singh's life is changing after his marriage? Think about

● The things that he says

● The things that he does

For a C grade: show a clear understanding of the things Singh says about himself and other people and give specific examples of his behaviour.

For an A grade: make sure you show how love blinds Singh to some of the things that the reader can see. You should also comment on the impact of the **imagery** the poet uses and explain how the carefully chosen structure conveys ideas to the reader.

Key contexts

ETHNIC DIVERSITY

The poems in this cluster cover a broad span of British history, including poems from three different centuries. We can see how English literature is changing as it reflects the increasing ethnic diversity of our society. Poems with origins in England, Wales, Scotland and Ireland are included and there are two poems which speak in different voices. In 'Checking Out Me History', the Caribbean voice of poet John Agard demanding recognition for the rich history of his people can be clearly heard. He makes us consider how limited our view of the past can be.

In Daljit Nagra's 'Singh Song!' the language is also obviously accented. We listen to an Indian voice talking to us. Both poems introduce a real immediacy because of this. It helps you to connect with a different way of looking at the world.

THE DISADVANTAGED

Characters who are disadvantaged provide a different perspective of our world and, by challenging our preconceptions, make us question our attitudes. Look at the voice of the homeless person in Simon Armitage's 'Give' who is prepared to force their way into our lives, to demand a change in our attitude to the homeless. Dylan Thomas shows a respectful sympathy for the hunchback who sits in the park all day, dreaming of friendship and companionship. Alison in U. V. Fanthorpe's poem inspires our sympathy because of the injury that stole her future from her. She became a person divided in half but neither part is complete and they no longer connect.

Betjeman's father was also disadvantaged because of his deafness but he built a happy and fulfilled life in spite of it. This makes his death seem so much harder to deal with for the poet. In 'The Ruined Maid' we see a woman who has been determined to leave all her disadvantages behind, to the envy of her more cautious friend who still lives in rural poverty. In 'The Clown Punk', however, the character disadvantages himself through his decisions and the poet shows him little sympathy as a result.

> **KEY QUOTE**
>
> 'vee stare past di half-price window signs at di beaches ov di UK in di brightey moon.'

> **KEY CONNECTIONS**
>
> Robert Allen Zimmerman changed his name as a tribute to his hero Dylan Thomas. He became Bob Dylan.

EXAMINER'S TIP: WRITING ABOUT KEY CONTEXTS

The poems have been brought together in a cluster called *Character and Voice* to reflect the richness of our culture and our heritage. They deal with different people with different problems and from different backgrounds. An examiner will always want to see detailed analysis of the poems in your answer but the fact that they exist within the context of *Character and Voice* already provides a link between them, which is something that would help you in your introduction or as you move from one poem to another.

Key themes

CHANGE

The most important **theme** that unites all the poems in this cluster is the idea of change. It might be regretted or welcomed. It might be necessary or cruel. But each of the voices here deals with change of some kind.

There are distressing physical changes that take place in Betjeman's father once he has died. There is no choice about this, for death is inevitable. The clown punk, however, has changed himself, foolishly it seems; Alison has been changed by an injury. Neither of those things can ever be undone. The hunchback yearns for change too but we know it is impossible for him to meet the fantasy figure he has created 'Straight and tall from his crooked bones'.

There are changes in the way **characters** are perceived. In 'Les Grands Seigneurs', Dorothy Molloy becomes 'a plaything', her previous influence now lost. This links to 'Ozymandias' by Shelley. Ozymandias's power and influence have been reduced to nothing more than a neglected broken statue. His boastful words are now empty and irrelevant. Amelia in Thomas Hardy's poem has made a huge change in her life and whatever the implications of her lifestyle choice, it has certainly changed the material aspects of her life.

In 'Brendon Gallacher' a toy is turned into an imaginary person and then back into a toy. Of course he is more than that. He is a symbol of childhood innocence that is suddenly shattered. The speaker's life will never be the same once he has been taken away. The little girl controlled him when he was her fantasy and there is a similar element of control in 'My Last Duchess'. When his wife no longer pleases him, the duke changes her from a person into an object, a picture on a wall, access to which only he can control.

Some poets demand change such as Simon Armitage in 'Give' and John Agard in 'Checking Out Me History' but in other poems, characters such as the horse whisperer don't want it. His role and reason for life is taken away from him by the introduction of the tractor. The river god in Stevie Smith's poem is a victim of the way people's perceptions have changed. Although he is neglected, he likes to reassert his power in his search for love and happiness. But he cannot change the woman he has drowned. He might be immortal but she is not and he can never remove the fear from her face.

Medusa discovers anger and a sense of revenge. The suspicions in her mind have taken physical form and turned into 'filthy snakes' on her head. Love has changed. This is 'Love gone bad'.

EXAMINER'S TIP: WRITING ABOUT CHANGE

This is a very wide-ranging theme that covers all the poems in the cluster. If you write about change, limit your material. Select some poems that you know well, so you can focus in depth on this broad theme, and access the highest marks. Remember that the poems deal with different aspects of change.

LOVE

Love is a defining human emotion. It drives many of the characters in the poems and shapes their lives. The river god seeks it; the hunchback imagines it; Medusa is hurt by it; the speaker in 'Les Grands Seigneurs' is confused by it.

Sometimes love is fragile. In 'Brendon Gallacher', the speaker's love for Brendon Gallacher is destroyed by a casual word by her mother. Her carefully created fantasy crumbles in a moment and she can never bring it back. In 'The River God' the immortal god looks for love but he can never stop people being frightened of him. He cannot change the expression on their faces. He destroys those he hopes to love. Medusa is frightening too and destructive. The difference is that she knows what she is doing.

For 'The Ruined Maid' her body is a commodity; the material benefits of her lifestyle seem the most important elements, which help to compensate for the shame of her adopted lifestyle. Material things are also important for the duke in 'My Last Duchess'. This is shown in the way he talks about the dowry before he talks about his bride. For both of them, money is most important because of the things it will buy.

Love transforms Singh's life. He worships his wife and neglects his duties, yet he is blind to her unhappiness. It is love that has made him blind. But love can be a dangerous emotion too. Her betrayal and need for revenge gives Medusa huge strength. She draws the life out of things and turns them to stone whilst she waits for the lover who wronged her to arrive. Her 'bride's breath soured'. In 'Les Grands Seigneurs', the speaker's love is a journey from freedom to subservience.

KEY QUOTE

'there are no Gallachers at 24 Novar'

EXAMINER'S TIP

Don't just write about the events in the poems. You need to write about the skill of the poet in exploring a particular theme or idea through the events.

THE PAST

Some of the **characters** in these poems yearn to return to the past because in the past they were happy. You can see this in 'The Horse Whisperer' and in 'Alison', where she looks at her photograph and sees her potential frozen and lost. The clown punk has also managed to lock himself into a past from which he will never escape, because he will be forever labelled by his markings.

Amelia in 'The Ruined Maid' has to confront her past when she meets her old friend. She certainly does not seem to regret what she has done. She made the decision to change her future and she can see her past when she listens to her previous life being described.

John Agard in 'Checking Out Me History' recognises how important an awareness of your own past can be. It defines a people and shows them the achievements of their ancestors. He suggests that without that you are suppressed and you lose your self-belief because you have lost your heritage.

The **theme** of the past provides a contrast that the poet can exploit. We see the difference between what once was and what is now. Look at Thomas Hardy's poem. Betjeman's poem is a good example too, since the contrast between then and now is shown in the way the poem is constructed. The sadness comes from the fact that we can never go back and change anything or stop it happening.

Progress and revision check

Revision activity

1. Name two poems which feature disadvantaged characters. (Write your answers below)

   ....

2. In which two poems is love regarded as a commodity?

   ....

3. Name two poets whose poems demand change.

   ....

4. Which two characters are shown to be physically frozen in time?

   ....

Revision activity

On a piece of paper write down answers to these questions:

- Write about two poems in which destructive aspects of love are explored.

  Start: *Both 'The River God' and 'Medusa' show that love does not always bring happiness. Medusa says…*

- Write about 'Ozymandias' and another poem in which power and influence have disappeared.

  Start: *'Les Grands Seigneurs' shows how the persona's life changed. Just like Ozymandias she once had…*

GRADE BOOSTER

Answer this longer, practice question about the key theme of change.

Q: Sometimes a person's life can be changed in a moment. Write about both 'Casehistory: Alison (head injury)' and 'The Horse Whisperer' which deal with life-changing moments.

For a C grade: explain clearly the reasons why the community turn on the horse whisperer and how Alison has become separated from her past and support your points with relevant evidence.

For an A grade: make sure you show how both characters are trapped and cannot return to the past. Show how the subtle differences in language and structure illustrate this. The horse whisperer's act of revenge was a final futile gesture. He is no longer needed. How does he speak about people? How does he speak about the horses? Alison looks at her photograph as if it is a different person, with doomed hopes and dreams. How does Alison talk about herself? Write about the sense of loss that links the two poems.

Here are a range of useful terms to know when writing about the cluster, what they mean and examples from the poems.

Literary term	Means?	Example
Irony	Deliberately saying one thing with the intention of having the opposite effect.	When Ozymandias says 'Look on my works, ye Mighty, and despair'.
Metaphor	When one thing is used to describe another.	When Dorothy Molloy says 'Men were my performing seals', she indicates the level of control she had over them.
Monologue	When a character speaks alone without interruption.	We hear Alison's thoughts and regrets in her own words.
Rhyme	When the last sounds of two or more words are similar or identical.	Look at how John Agard uses rhyme to contrast European and Caribbean history.

THE WORDS POETS USE

Poets work by selecting every word with great care. In 'Les Grands Seigneurs' you can see that each word carries an echo or a suggestion. Look at the duke in 'My Last Duchess'. He doesn't say that his wife upsets him or made him cross. He uses the word 'disgust'. It is an extreme word and it suggests extreme behaviour.

Words are selected for reasons. They reveal **character**. Look at Medusa. She comments on herself in very simple language. The sentences are short and the language is simple because she abandoned all complexity when she was betrayed. She is aware of how she is being transformed. All she wants now is revenge. Look at the effect and the implications of the words 'yellow fanged' from the second verse. They have an animal association. She seems to be losing all her humanity and becoming a predator. An **atmosphere** is created by the words selected in all the poems in this cluster.

Why does Singh's wife wear 'high heels' in 'Singh Song!'? There must be a reason why Daljit Nagra included this detail. When we ask ourselves that, we bring our own perspective to the poem and form a more complex impression of her character.

There is interesting use of **diction** in Andrew Forster's 'The Horse Whisperer'. He maintained his status through mysterious words and spells. This contrasts with the practicality of tractors. When the horse whisperer ran away, he says that he joined 'the stampede'. This word links directly with the horses he used to care for, as well as indicating the huge change that happened in the community.

In 'Checking Out Me History', John Agard uses words that describe the hidden figures from history as heroic. He uses words such as 'vision', 'see-far' and 'sunrise', the latter suggesting a beginning. This adds to the idea in the poem that these significant people are being neglected.

GRADE BOOSTER

Always remember that the poet wrote their work because they had something important to say. Never think for a moment that they wrote what they did so that it could appear in an examination.

Look too at the way the choice of words in 'Give' set up important echoes in our minds which adds depth to a short poem in an extremely effective way.

Rhymes are more than just a musical chime. They serve an important purpose in giving emphasis to particular words. You can see this in 'The River God', where the rhyme between 'drowning' and 'clowning' is a significant indication of the river god's character.

HOW POETS VARY LINE AND SENTENCE LENGTH FOR EFFECT

Variation in sentence length or line length are important aspects of a poet's style. Short sentences can give a real impact. There is an excellent example in 'Ozymandias', 'Nothing else remains', which is the most important comment of all on the arrogance of the dead king.

The use of short sentences provides a significant insight into the tragedy that Alison represents in 'Casehistory: Alison (head injury)'. 'Brendon Gallacher' ends with a short sentence which captures perfectly the bereavement that the speaker had suffered, 'Oh my Brendon Gallacher'.

In 'My Last Duchess' the long, flowing sentences reflect the character of the duke. He appears cultured and thoughtful. We are carried along by what he says, particularly because of the **enjambment** that puts less emphasis on the rhymes. As a result, the short sentence in which he says 'I gave commands' comes as a shock.

THE WAY POETS USE IMAGERY TO ENHANCE THEIR MESSAGE

The images and comparisons poets use give us insight. Look at 'Hunchback in the Park'. The hunchback returns to the park every day where he can set his mind free. Examine the image of the water cup. It represents the hunchback, who is chained **metaphorically** to the park. The poet even imagines him chained in a kennel when he goes home. When the boys fill the cup with gravel, they are abusing him; when the poet sailed his toy boat in the fountain, it is a symbol of the freedom that the hunchback is denied.

Look at the effect of comparing the clown punk with a basket of washing. It creates a picture of randomly selected clothes chosen with no plan. It reflects the kind of comic figure that he has become. The punk part of him once represented challenge and intimidation, which is seen in his tattoos. But as his clothes suggest, he has actually become a clown.

Dorothy Molloy's use of **metaphor** is an essential part of 'Les Grands Seigneurs'. Each association made is important, each one adds to our understanding. Look at the end of the poem when all that complex **imagery** disappears and is replaced by very straightforward language when she is married. There is a clear conclusion to be drawn.

The images used in 'Medusa' show the mental state of the character. There is a sense of destruction that is growing in her; living things are turned instantly to stone, the life drained from them just as she has been drained of love.

GRADE BOOSTER

You analyse and 'decode' a poem in order to improve your understanding of the poet's work. But always remember that the poem should be regarded as something complete in itself.

KEY QUOTE

'Like a basket of washing that got up and walked'

KEY CONNECTIONS

Highgate Cemetery was opened in 1839 on a hillside with excellent views of London, enjoyed by Betjeman's father. It contains the graves of many famous people including that of Karl Marx. Betjeman himself is buried in Cornwall.

THE WAY POETS USE CONTRAST TO CREATE EFFECTS

Poets use contrasts in order to compare one idea with another and so increase the emotional impact on the reader. Look at the contrasts in 'The Ruined Maid', for example in the conversation between the two women.

Look also at 'On a Portrait of a Deaf Man' where Betjeman carefully contrasts the past and the present not only within the language but also within the structure of the verse itself. His father might have liked to shake hands with his friends before he died but now we are told that his finger bones 'Stick through his finger ends'. This pattern of moving from life to death is present throughout the poem.

There are important contrasts too in 'The River God' which are established through the use of language. There is a contrast between the condition of the river itself which is smelly and untidy and the golden hair of the drowned woman. Her beauty is so out of place in the world of the river god that he must tie her down with weeds.

THE VOICES THAT POETS USE

All poems are conversations or dialogues. Sometimes they are between different **characters** as we see in 'The Ruined Maid'. This enables the poet to establish character. As a result, we see that Amelia actually says very little. It is her excited old friend who talks. What does that tell us about Amelia? That perhaps she has a superior attitude to the woman she left behind and has little to say to her? That she doesn't want to voice her regrets about the decision she has made? That she does not care what others think? All this achieved in very few words.

Often these poems are a conversation between the poet or his creation and the reader. As such, they are very successful. In 'Casehistory; Alison (head injury)' and 'The Horse Whisperer', we hear characters tell us their own tragic stories. As first person **narrative**, they have impact and inspire sympathy. There is a sense that we are getting the innermost thoughts of the characters. These two examples both reflect on the pain inflicted by the passage of time.

Poets also create character by capturing what people say and the way in which they say it. In 'Brendon Gallacher', Jackie Kay has created an impression of a child's voice by using repetition very effectively.

The great triumph of the dramatic **monologue** is 'My Last Duchess', a remarkable piece of writing, with structure, control and psychological insight. We find out everything about the duke in his own words. He reveals himself as a cold hearted killer at the same time as he is telling us how sophisticated he is.

We reveal ourselves in the things we say and the characters here are created in their own words. Look at Ozymandias's words. It is the contrast between the arrogance of the 'King of Kings' and the reality of the desolation which surrounds him that stands out. The sands are 'lone and level'. This is one of the great English poems and it is remembered precisely because of the poetic devices of voice and contrast.

KEY QUOTE

'I was the life-blood no longer'

EXAMINER'S TIP

When we hear a character speak, we draw conclusions about them. But they may not be necessarily telling the truth. So make a judgement.

Progress and revision check

Revision activity

❶ Identify one detail in 'Singh Song!' which might suggest that the wife is dissatisfied with her life? (Write your answers below)

....

❷ Give two examples of poems that achieve an effect by using short sentences.

....

❸ In which poem does the poet achieve important contrasts by using the device of conversation?

....

❹ Which poet uses repetition to suggest a child's language?

....

❺ Which character is associated with a chained drinking cup?

....

Revision activity

On a piece of paper write down answers to these questions:

● Write about the way language can emphasise a character's mental state.

Start: *The imagery Carol Ann Duffy uses in Medusa is a perfect example of the character's mental state. She…*

● Write about a poem in which a poet uses **rhyme** effectively.

Start: *In 'The River God' Stevie Smith uses rhyme very successfully. At the beginning of the poem…*

GRADE BOOSTER ★

Answer this longer, practice question about the words that poets use:

Q: Give examples of how poets in this cluster select words carefully to achieve their effects. Think about…

● How Betjeman and Duffy select their vocabulary to create unpleasant images. Why do they do this?

● The way in which Simon Armitage uses words in 'Give' to add depth to the poem.

For a C grade: show a clear understanding of the way the unhappiness of the voices is revealed. Show that the idea of death is central to Betjeman and Duffy. Refer to the religious vocabulary in 'Give'.

For an A grade: make sure you show how Armitage gives his poem universality by linking it to the Nativity. Show how decay is a central idea. Write about how the idea of change links Betjeman and Duffy.

PART FIVE: GRADE BOOSTER

Understanding the question

Questions in exams or controlled conditions often need **'decoding'**. Decoding helps to ensure that your answer is relevant and refers to what you have been asked.

 ## UNDERSTAND EXAM LANGUAGE

Get used to exam and essay style language by looking at specimen questions and the words they use. For example:

Exam speak!	Means?	Example 'Checking Out Me History' by John Agard
'convey ideas'	*'get across a point to the reader'* Usually you have to say *'how'* this is done.	The use of details from nursery rhymes conveys to the reader the idea that much of the history he has been taught is trivial.
'methods, techniques, ways'	The *'things'* the writer does – such as a powerful description, a shocking event, which he reveals, how someone speaks.	The poet uses metaphors in the verses about the people from Black history to emphasise their heroism and nobility.
'present, represent'	1) present: *'the way things are told to us'* 2) represent: *'what those things might mean underneath'*	Agard *presents* the reader with a contrast between different versions of history. This *represents* the idea that his people have been oppressed.

 ## 'BREAK DOWN' THE QUESTION

Pick out the key words or phrases. For example:

Question: 'Compare how a **character's voice** is created in 'The River God' and **one** other poem from *Characters and Voices*.

● The focus is on **'character's voice'**, so you will need to talk about the **river god**, what he/she, says and how he/she is described, and the same for another poem's character/voice.

● The word **'compare'** tells us this is a question which is asking you to look at two poems and look for connections and differences in how the voices are presented.

What does this tell you?

● **focus on the voices** (how the language is used to convey character and feeling) not so much on the themes and ideas (although these are bound to come up, too).

 ## KNOW YOUR LITERARY LANGUAGE!

When studying texts you will come across words such as theme, issue, idea, symbol, imagery, metaphor. Some of these words could come up in the exam question. Make sure you know what they mean before you write your answer!

Comparing poems

Comparing poems is a **key skill** which requires **careful thought**. Some of the skills you need are general ones, useful for any comparison work; others are specific to poetry.

When comparing **two** poems, you will need to:

- Comment on **points of similarity** and **points of difference**.

- Write about the **overall subject** of the **question** (i.e. the theme of conflict) but focus on the **different aspects** of **each poem** (language, structure, voice, etc.).

- Write in a **logical**, **structured way** that makes your ideas **clear** and **easy to follow** (use linking words and phrases, such as 'but' and 'however', to guide the examiner through what you say).

- Try to come up with your own **individual interpretation** or thoughts.

HOW TO START: A GOOD INTRODUCTION

You could begin with a general introduction comparing the two poems. For example:

The poets of 'Medusa' and 'Singh Song!' both convey quite different attitudes to conflict through the way **they tell their stories**, the **language used**, and the **structures** they adopt.

This introduction then gives you the chance to deal with **each of these aspects** in turn.

DEVELOPING THE COMPARISON: WRITE A PARAGRAPH FOR EACH POINT

Here is an example in which the same point is explored with regard to both poems:

Both poems explore different aspects of love through the voice of a character. Medusa and Singh speak to us directly about their feelings in their own voices. Medusa is aware that she is changing as a result of her betrayal. Her love has become destructive and it has given her dangerous powers. Singh has **also** changed as a result of his love. He neglects his duties and devotes his time to his wife. **In his case**, however, he is not so aware. Love has made him blind to the world around him.

First sentence introduces the idea that this paragraph will deal with this aspect

Comparative phrase links both poems

Contrast phrase links both poems

PERSONAL INTERPRETATION

You can add your own views at any point, but the key is to think **'outside the box'**. For example, you *could* say: 'Is it possible that that Nagra wishes to present Singh as a man who will eventually be very unhappy when he faces up to the reality of the woman he has married?'

EXAMINER'S TIP

Dealing in turn with each aspect in both poems is a high-level skill which will show your ability to compare and contrast. If this is too challenging, you can write about *each poem in turn*, but you must make comparative and contrasting comments as you go along.

Dealing with an 'unseen' poem

This aspect of the written exam may seem daunting. But it is an opportunity to show off your **creative thinking** and **analytical skills**.

 ## ADAPT TO SURVIVE!

Normally, you would be able to **annotate** a poem (underline key words, write questions, highlight phrases, etc.) but in the written exam *you are not allowed to do this*. The instructions state:

- Do not annotate the poems.
- Write any rough work in your answer book.
- Cross out anything you don't wish to be marked.

This is fine. All you need to do is:

- Read the poem in the exam paper once or twice without writing anything.
- Then, write notes about the poem in your answer book.
- Put a heading 'Notes' so that you know to cross these out later.

 ## KEEP IT SIMPLE

- Start your notes by quickly jotting down what you think the **'story'** of the poem is. This could be as simple as: 'the poet talks about a river and what he sees' OR, 'the poet expresses his feelings about his father'.
- Then, as you would if you were annotating the poem itself, jot down *very quickly* the key things you notice about:
  - The **structure** (verses, patterns, repetitions, rhyme/sound, etc.).
  - Key powerful **words/phrases** (don't write them out, just put a line reference – i.e. line 2: strong metaphor).
  - Anything related to the question itself (does it mention a **theme** or **idea**?).

Don't take any more than five minutes for this. You **only have 30 minutes** for the whole answer.

 ## STICK TO WHAT THE POET DOES AND THE EFFECT

Almost certainly your question will be about how the poet *presents* an idea, so in your answer think of making 4–5 points about how the poet makes his point, presents his idea, tells his story. One point for each paragraph.

Planning your answer

It is vital that you plan your response to the controlled assessment task or possible exam question carefully, and that you then follow your plan, if you are to gain the higher grades.

 **ANNOTATE AND ORGANISE**

When revising for the exam, or planning your response to the controlled assessment task, make **notes** on particular aspects of the poems you have highlighted, so that you have a **'ready reference'** for comparison, revision or planning purposes. For example, you might list ideas as shown below for the poem 'Give':

Key point/aspect	Evidence (quotation, reference to structure, etc.)	The effect this has or the idea conveyed
A powerful and insistent voice	'Of all the public places, dear To make a scene, I've chosen here.'	It makes the reader feel that they are being addressed directly by a homeless person.

 **EXAMINER'S TIP**

Be ready to write about any of the poems. You never know what the question might be.

PLAN FOR PARAGRAPHS

Use paragraphs to plan your answer.

❶ The first paragraph should **introduce** the **argument** you wish to make.

❷ Then, jot down how the paragraphs that follow will **develop** this argument with **details**, **examples** and other possible **points of view**. Each paragraph is likely to deal with one point at a time.

❸ **Sum up** your argument in the last paragraph.

For example, for the following task:

Question: Compare how attitudes to death are shown in 'On a Portrait of a Deaf Man' and one other poem from *Character and Voice*.

Simple plan:
Paragraph 1: Introduction
Paragraph 2: First point – *explore attitudes to death in 'On a Portrait of a Deaf Man' and make point about the way that Betjeman cannot see beyond the decay of the body or accept the existence of the soul.*
Paragraph 3: Second point – *further comment on attitudes in 'On a Portrait of a Deaf Man' and related points about the way Betjeman contrasts how his father was when alive with how he imagines him now he is dead.*
Paragraph 4: Third point – *explore attitudes to death in other poems from the cluster e.g. 'The River God'.*
Paragraph 5: Fourth point – *make new point about attitudes to death in 'The River God'.*
Paragraph 6: Conclusion – *draw together what you want to say about the theme across the two poems.*

How to use quotations

One of the secrets of success in writing essays is to use quotations **effectively**. There are five basic principles:

❶ Put quotation marks at the beginning and end of the quotation.

❷ Write the quotation exactly as it appears in the original.

❸ Do not use a quotation that repeats what you have just written.

❹ Use the quotation so that it fits into your sentence or, if it is longer, indent it as a separate paragraph.

❺ Only quote what is most useful.

 **USE QUOTATIONS TO DEVELOP YOUR ARGUMENT**

Quotations should be used to developv the line of thought in your essays. Your comment should not duplicate what is in your quotation. Look at this example taken from 'Casehistory: Alison (head injury)':

GRADE D/E GRADE C

(simply repeats the idea)	(makes point and supports with a relevant quotation)
Alison looks at her photograph and says that the person in the picture knew things that made her smile which she now cannot remember. '…Her face, broken By nothing sharper than smiles, holds in its smiles What I have forgotten.'	Alison looks at her photograph and realises that when it was taken she hadn't experienced suffering because she says that her face 'Holds in its smiles / What I have forgotten.'

However the most sophisticated way of using the writer's words is to embed them into your sentence, and further develop the point:

GRADE A

(makes point, embeds quote and develops idea)
Alison realises that in the photograph she appears innocent and that her face 'holds in its smiles' experiences and memories that 'I have forgotten.' The use of the possessive 'its' and 'I' emphasises the two different Alisons from the past and the present.

When you use quotations in this way, you are demonstrating the ability to use text as evidence to support your ideas – not simply including words from the original to prove you have read it.

 **EXAMINER'S TIP**

Try using a quotation to begin your response. You can use it as a launch pad for your ideas, or as an idea you are going to argue against.

★ **GRADE BOOSTER**

Where appropriate, refer to the language technique used and the effect it creates. For example, if you say, 'this metaphor shows how…', or 'the effect of this metaphor is to emphasise to the reader…' this will get you much higher marks.

Sitting the examination

Examination papers are carefully designed to give you the opportunity to do your best. Follow these handy hints for exam success:

 BEFORE YOU START

- Make sure that you **know the poems** you are writing about so that you are properly prepared and equipped. If you are preparing for an **'unseen'** poem, make sure you have **practised** relevant **techniques** to succeed.
- You need to be **comfortable** and **free from distractions**. Inform the invigilator if anything is off-putting, e.g. a shaky desk.
- **Read** and follow the instructions, or rubric, on the front of the examination paper. You should know by now what you need to do but **check** to reassure yourself.
- Before beginning your answer have a **skim** through the **whole paper** to make sure you don't miss anything **important**.
- Observe the **time allocation** – and follow it carefully. If they recommend 45 minutes for a particular question on a text, make sure this is how long you spend.

 WRITING YOUR RESPONSES

A typical 45 minutes examination essay is between 550 and 800 words long.

Ideally, spend a minimum of 5 minutes planning your answer before you begin.

Use the questions to structure your response. Here is an example:

Question: Compare how a character's voice is created in 'The River God' and **one** other poem from *Character and Voice*.

- The introduction to your answer could briefly describe the **two poems** and the 'story' they tell.
- The second part could explain the **voice in 'The River God'** and how it is created.
- The third part could explore the **voice in the second poem** you select, possibly linking back to 'The River God'.
- The conclusion would **sum up your own viewpoint**, mentioning the key aspects of each poem.

For each part allocate paragraphs to cover the points you wish to make (see **Planning your answer**).

Keep your writing legible and easy to read, using paragraphs and link words to show the structure of your answers.

Spend a couple of minutes afterwards quickly checking for obvious errors.

 'KEY WORDS' ARE THE KEY!

Keep on mentioning the **key words** from the question in your answer. This will keep you on track and remind the examiner that you are answering the question set.

> **EXAMINER'S TIP**
>
> Arrive in plenty of time for the exam. Don't arrive so late that you have no time to relax before you enter the room.

> ★ **GRADE BOOSTER**
>
> What emotions inspired the poets in this selection? Were they angry? Amused? Unhappy? Understanding what inspired them will help you achieve a greater understanding.

Sitting the controlled assessment

It may be the case that you are responding to 'Brendon Gallacher' in a controlled assessment situation. Follow these useful tips for success.

 WHAT YOU ARE REQUIRED TO DO

Make sure you are clear about:

● The **specific text** and **task** you are preparing (is it on just one poem or several poems from this cluster?)

● How **long** you have during the assessment period (i.e. 3–4 hours?)

● How **much** you are expected or allowed to write (i.e. 2,000 words?)

● **What** you are allowed to **take** into the controlled assessment, and what you can use (or not, as the case may be!) You may be able to take in brief notes but not draft answers, so check with your teacher.

 HOW YOU CAN PREPARE

> **EXAMINER'S TIP**
>
> At least one poem you write about must be a 'Literary Heritage' poem, and one must be contemporary (modern).

Once you know your task, topic and text/s you can:

● Make **notes** and **prepare** the **points, evidence, quotations,** etc. you are likely to use.

● **Practise** or draft **model answers**.

● Use these **York Notes** to hone your **skills**, e.g. use of quotations, how to plan an answer and focus on what makes a **top grade**.

 DURING THE CONTROLLED ASSESSMENT

Remember:

● **Stick** to the **topic** and task you have been given.

● The allocated **time** is for **writing**, so make the most of it. It is **double** the time you might have in an exam, so you will be writing **almost twice** as much (or more) although you *may* also be writing on a larger number of poems, probably at least four.

● At the end of the controlled assessment follow your teacher's **instructions**. For example, make sure you have written your name **clearly** on all the pages you hand in.

Improve your grade

It is useful to know the type of responses examiners are looking for when they award different grades. The following broad guidance should help you to improve your grade when responding to the task you are set!

GRADE C

What you need to show	What this means
Sustained response to task and text	You write enough! You don't run out of ideas after two paragraphs.
Effective use of **details** to **support** your **explanations**	You generally support what you say with evidence, i.e. *The river god seems both simple and sly, saying he is 'old' and 'smelly' but at the same time playing with drowning figures in the water.*
Explanation of effects of writer's **use of language**, structure, form, etc., and the **effect on readers**	You must write about the writer's use of these things. It's not enough simply to give a viewpoint. So, you might comment on the way a poet uses a final couplet to emphasise a point, or a powerful image to stress and idea, such as the pieces of a statue scattered across the empty desert.
Appropriate comment on **characters, plots, themes, ideas** and **settings**	What you say is relevant; if the task asks you to comment on how a setting is shown, that is what you write about.

GRADE A

What you need to show *in addition* to the above	What this means
Insightful, exploratory response to the text	You look beyond the obvious; you might see the duke in 'My Last Duchess' as a man incapable of love who wishes to control those around him. He likes art because it never changes. His young wife showed that she had an independent spirit which he found threatening. So he turned her into a picture which he could hide from or show to others as he saw fit.
Close analysis and use of **detail**	If you are looking at the writer's use of language, you might comment on each word in a line, drawing out its distinctive effect on the reader; i.e. in 'Medusa' commenting on how 'foul mouthed' can refer both to cursing and to a bad taste left by her relationships, and 'yellow fanged' suggests both the snake's bite and, in a more modern sense, old, smoke-coloured teeth suggesting her beauty has diminished.
Convincing and **imaginative interpretation**	Your viewpoint is likely to convince the examiner. You show you have 'engaged' with the text, and come up with your own ideas. These may be based on what you have discussed in class or read about, but you have made your own decisions.

Annotated sample answers

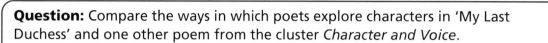

This section will provide you with extracts from two model answers, one at **C grade** and one at **A grade**, to give you an idea of what is required to achieve at different levels.

> **Question:** Compare the ways in which poets explore characters in 'My Last Duchess' and one other poem from the cluster *Character and Voice*.

CANDIDATE 1

In this essay I am going to look at characters in two poems, 'My Last Duchess' by Robert Browning and 'The Ruined Maid' by Thomas Hardy. These poems have similarities because you can hear the characters speaking to you directly.

Good start – context established

'My Last Duchess' is written as a dramatic monologue. No one else speaks, but we can build up a picture of his character from the things that he says. He has murdered his wife and is prepared to talk about it calmly as if it was not a crime. He assumes that the envoy who he is speaking to will agree with him. We can see how he feels in the language that he uses. He says that her behaviour 'disgusts' him, which shows that he has a vicious character. He loves art and beautiful things and he treated his wife as one of his possessions. When he didn't want her any more, he got rid of her. I think he is suspicious of her behaviour.

Who does this refer to?

Pleasing comments made – avoids telling the story

Well-chosen quotation and supportive comment, referring back to the title

On the other hand, 'The Ruined Maid' is a conversation between two old friends who have met in the street. They used to live in the same village but their lives have been very different. Amelia left to become a prostitute because she couldn't stand life in the village any longer because they were so poor.

An effective link which takes the reader into the next section

'You used to call home-life a hag-ridden dream.'

Amelia is now dressed in much better clothes and her life seems less hard.

We can see her character in her replies. She is the one who talks about being ruined. It makes her sound confident and proud that she took a decision. She has had to pay a big price for all this but she thinks it is worth it and her friend is envious because her life is so hard.

Could make a clearer link to the importance of possessions in 'My Last Duchess'

An interesting comment about character based on language she uses – needs an example

Who is this paragraph about? Not very clear

Overall comment: This essay is clearly written and addresses the question. Limited but well-chosen quotations are used. Good points are made, although they are not always developed. It would have been better to compare the poems side by side rather than deal with them in two separate sections. Needs more on 'My Last Duchess'.

GRADE C

CANDIDATE 2

A clear and confident opening focusing on the question

Clear transition to Hardy's poem – this happens throughout the answer

Important conclusion drawn

Why would her friend concentrate on material things?

The answer ends with comments which show personal involvement with the texts

The two poems, 'My Last Duchess' by Robert Browning and 'The Ruined Maid' by Thomas Hardy, present character in a successful and interesting way. In both cases the reader can see how a character is revealed in what they say, rather than through description or comment.

The poets let the characters speak for themselves. Indeed in 'My Last Duchess' the duke is all you hear. The fact that duke doesn't require a reply from the envoy underlines his arrogance. He expects to talk and he expects others to listen. In 'The Ruined Maid' Hardy reveals the characters of two women through their conversation and in so doing makes a clear point about the consequences of rural poverty. One character is excited and envious when she meets her friend who escaped from 'a hag-ridden dream' and found a more comfortable life through prostitution. Hardy does not explore the consequences of this decision except through the eyes of her friend who comments entirely upon material things, since these are the things that her lifestyle denies her. The Ruined Maid herself speaks with confidence drawing attention to her new status.

'One's pretty lively when ruined, said she.'

When you consider the material aspects of their different life styles, you do question which one is ruined.

The duke seems concerned with material things too. One of his possessions was his wife. He regarded her as something that should have reflected his status, not as an individual. We form an impression of her through the poet's choice of words he gives to the duke to speak. She appears playful and lively and inspires strong feelings of devotion from those around her. One brings her a 'bough of cherries.' There is a contrast between the devotion this implies and the reaction of her husband. The duke says that her behaviour 'disgusts me'. What seems particularly revealing is that he seems more interested in the dowry his next duchess will bring than in her as a person. It strikes the reader as particularly chilling that he sees nothing wrong with the murder of a wife who did not fulfil his expectations. In both poems love is disregarded. Emotions and relationships are commodities to be traded.

Good comment. What about his need to control? The portrait? Perhaps a quotation would help

Excellent example of an embedded quotation

These comments on the duchess are an important aspect to this answer

Overall comment: The essay moves confidently between the two texts. It uses well-chosen quotations and draws conclusions about character. It is well argued and fluent. It shows awareness of the poet's intention. The structure of the verse and the effect it has should have been explored, particularly in 'My Last Duchess'.

GRADE A

Further questions

EXAM-STYLE QUESTIONS

If you are studying *Unit 2: Poetry Across Time*, you will have a written examination of 75 minutes worth 54 marks. There are 36 marks for a question based on the poetry cluster, *Character and Voice*. The other 18 marks will be awarded for your response to a poem you may not have seen before.

You are advised to spend 45 minutes on your answer to the question based on poems in the cluster. You will be asked to compare one named poem with another poem chosen by yourself from the cluster you have studied.

Here are some examples of the sort of questions you could be asked:

❶ Examine the ways that two poets have written about the past. Compare 'The Horse Whisperer' with one other poem from the cluster *Character and Voice*.

❷ John Betjeman expresses his anger at the death of his father in 'On a Portrait of a Deaf Man'. Compare this poem with another from the cluster which expresses strong emotion.

❸ Compare the way that 'Checking Out Me History' calls for a change in attitudes with another poem from the cluster *Character and Voice*.

❹ 'Singh Song!' tells a story in the character's own voice. Compare this poem with another from the cluster which uses the same technique.

❺ 'Brendon Gallacher' by Jackie Kay achieves important effects through repetition. Compare this poem with another poem from the cluster which uses repetition successfully.

CONTROLLED ASSESSMENT-STYLE QUESTIONS

If you are studying Unit 5: Exploring Poetry, you will be expected to complete a Controlled Assessment worth 40 marks over a period of 3–4 hours. If you have used the cluster *Character and Voice* for this unit, you could expect questions like these:

❶ Explore the different ways in which poets have given insight into characters in the texts you have studied.

❷ Explore the ways poets express strong, personally held views in the texts you have studied.

❸ Explore how poets deal with the way people change over time in the texts you have studied.

❹ Explore the ways in which the poets deal with love and anger in the texts you have studied.

❺ Explore why poets use striking visual imagery in the texts you have studied.

Literary terms

Literary term	Explanation
alliteration	Where the same sound is repeated in a stretch of language, usually at the beginnings of words
assonance	When the same sound appears in the same place in a series of words
atmosphere	A mood or feeling
blank verse	Unrhymed iambic pentameter
character(s)	Either a person in a poem, novel, play, etc. or his or her personality
chronological	When the events in a story are told in the order they happened. It is possible to have a chronological narrative containing flashbacks as long as the main narrative continues to move forwards through time
cliché	A word or phrase that has become boring and lost its meaning through over-use
colloquial	The everyday speech used by people in ordinary situations
connotation	An additional meaning attached to a word in specific circumstances, i.e. what it suggests or implies
couplet	A pair of rhymed lines of any metre
dialect	Accent and vocabulary, varying by region and social background
dialogue	A conversation between two or more characters; or the words spoken by characters in general
diction	The choice of words in a work of literature
enjambment	The continuation of a sentence without pause beyond the end of a line
iambic pentameter	A line of poetry consisting of five iambic feet
imagery	Descriptive language which uses images to make actions, objects and characters more vivid in the reader's mind. Metaphors and similes are examples of imagery
irony	When someone deliberately says one thing when they mean another, usually in a humorous or sarcastic way
metaphor	When one thing is used to describe another thing to create a striking or unusual image
monologue	A long speech delivered by one character
narrative	A story or tale and the particular way that it is told. First person narratives ('I') are told from the character's perspective and usually require the reader to judge carefully what is being said; second person narratives ('you') suggest the reader is part of the story; in third person narratives ('he, 'she', 'they'), the narrator may be intrusive (continually commenting on the story), impersonal (without their own personality or views), or omniscient. More than one style of narrative may be used in a text

Literary term	Explanation
narrator	The voice telling the story or relating a sequence of events
persona	An author's assumed character in his or her writing
rhyme	When the last sounds of two or more words are similar or identical
rhythm	In poetry or music, the pattern of stresses or beats in a line
simile	When one thing is compared directly to another thing, using the words 'like' or 'as'
soliloquy	When a character speaks directly to the audience as if thinking aloud, revealing their inner thoughts, feelings and intentions
symbolism	When an object, a person or a thing is used to represent another thing
theme	A central idea examined by an author / poet

Checkpoint answers

Checkpoint 1
'Medusa'.

Checkpoint 2
'The Hunchback in the Park'.

Checkpoint 3
'The Hunchback in the Park', 'On a Portrait of a Deaf Man' and 'Les Grands Seigneurs'.

Checkpoint 4
'Ozymandias'.

Checkpoint 5
'My Last Duchess'.

Checkpoint 6
'Les Grands Seigneurs' and 'My Last Duchess'.

Checkpoint 7
'The Hunchback in the Park', 'Brendon Gallacher'.

Checkpoint 8
'The Clown Punk'.

Checkpoint 9
'The Ruined Maid'.

Checkpoint 10
'Casehistory: Alison (head injury)'.